FORGING LEGACY

FORGING
BOOK 2

LAINEY DAVIS

By Lainey Davis

Join my newsletter and never miss a new release!

laineydavis.com

© 2024 Lainey Davis

All rights reserved. No portion of this book may be reproduced in any form without permission from the publisher, except as permitted by U.S. copyright law.

This is a work of fiction. Names, characters, business, events and incidents are the products of the author's imagination. Any resemblance to actual persons, living or dead, or actual events is purely coincidental.

Edited by Becky with Bookcase Media

ABOUT THE BOOK

Turns out my hot one night stand ... is my professor...

I don't do relationships, but when a gorgeous bartender presses her chest in my face on New Year's Eve, I take it as a sign that maybe I should bend my rules.

I've been under so much pressure lately, between my agent and my soccer prospects and my abusive biological father trying to extort money I don't even have.

What better way to distract myself from the pressures of going pro than to get under a woman whose curves could make a Venus statue jealous? Fern is everything a man could ask for: unbearably sexy, brilliantly witty, and oh-so-responsive in bed.

That unforgettable night was the best bad decision I've ever made. That is until she shows up as the TA in my math class. Suddenly, our forbidden connection could jeopardize both of our futures.

When I am exposed for my secret relationship with Fern and threaten her academic career, I'll do anything to protect her—even if it means giving up everything I've worked for.

To have a shot at happily ever after with the woman I love, I have to confront my painful past head-on and fight like hell to forge my own path. Can I break free from the shadows that haunt me and build a new life with Fern by my side? One thing's for sure - I've never wanted anything more.

CONTENT NOTE

This novel contains mentions and descriptions of parental abuse and neglect, which may be triggering for some readers. While not gratuitous in detail, the story does explore the long-lasting emotional and psychological impact of this trauma on the main character, Wyatt.

Please be advised that the following topics are discussed or alluded to within the narrative:

Physical and emotional abuse; Child endangerment and neglect; Manipulation and gaslighting; Anxiety, panic attacks, and PTSD; Unhealthy family dynamics and strained parent-child relationships

My intent is to handle these sensitive topics with care and respect while realistically portraying the challenges of overcoming past trauma. Please take care of yourself when reading.

CHAPTER 1
WYATT

I HAVE zero desire to drive my cousins to a crowded bar just to be their designated driver when they close the place down.

I have even less desire to deal with their nagging and whining, so I guess I'm showering and putting on some sort of decent clothing to leave the apartment. A rotating cast of my cousins has lived in this three-bedroom apartment for years as we worked our way through Pittsburgh University— where most of us are varsity athletes.

Which means when we get a night off from our nutrition plan, we make up for lost time. Or ... they do, anyway. I don't like losing control like that. I don't want to do something I'll regret. Something I can't undo.

"Yo, Wyatt! You curling your hair or what? We're missing happy hour." My cousin Odin pounds a fist on my bedroom door. I can hear Stellen and Gunnar grumbling behind him in the living room. I glance in the mirror and smooth a hand back through my dark hair. I cram a baseball cap down low, hoping it's enough to keep people from recognizing me. I really hate crowds.

With a sigh, I flick off the lights and pull the door open in a carefully timed maneuver that sets Odin off balance. I don't move to catch him as he stumbles into my room; we all laugh as he curses me from the floor. "You guys ready to go or what?" I ask, grabbing the keys to my Range Rover and striding toward the door.

Stellen argues his way into the front seat and turns on both his seat warmer and mine. It's New Year's Eve and cold as balls outside. Most of the students are still away for break, but half the sports teams have matches. We're going out with guys from the football and ice hockey teams. Which tends to mean there will be tons of girls looking to get lucky, rattling off our stats, and asking for damn autographs on bar napkins.

Did I mention I hate all this?

"Are you wearing perfume?" Odin leans front and sniffs my neck.

I swat him away. "Knock it off, man. It's called soap. I showered."

"Gunny, doesn't Wyatt smell like he's wearing a little something?" Soon all three of my cousins are sniffing me, sniffing themselves.

I try to ignore all of it and look for a parking spot near the bar. Something must be going right between me and karma because someone pulls out of a space a few doors down. All four of us cheer as I put on my blinker, hoping the scent analysis is finished.

Odin pulls out his shirt collar. He is, of course, not wearing a coat. He's like his dad, my Uncle Ty—a furnace.

Odin bucked all sorts of Stag family traditions and started playing football.

My mom and dad are deep into the world of pro soccer; Uncle Ty was a legendary pro hockey player.

Stellen's dad, my Uncle Tim, always preferred to boss everyone around—he's a sports lawyer who manages all their contracts.

Odin rubs his palms together and waits for the traffic to pass so he can open his door. "All right, men. Let the good times roll. I've got exactly twelve more hours to exercise my liver before I start training for the combine."

I chuckle. At least my coach gives us New Year's Day off, but then I'm a senior and I've got a different path to going pro in my sport. I'm more focused on working with my agent to get signed somewhere far from Pittsburgh. I need to get the hell away from the specter of my biological father.

My cousins walk ahead of me and into the bar, where a loud chorus of cheers erupts from the crowd of fellow athletes and sports fans. If I time things just right, I can slide in at the tail end of the ruckus and find a seat at the bar.

This is exactly what I do, tugging my hat down a bit lower and pulling my Aunt Emma's latest book from my jacket pocket to read. A bartender asks me what I'm having, and I grunt out a request for a soda. Aunt Emma wrote a significant nonfiction bestseller about sexism and the patriarchy in the world of professional soccer. My cousin's girlfriend, Cara, is part of the book because she got grabbed and kissed on international television by some jerk in the Soccer USA office.

I'm racing my way through a chapter about his eventual jail time when liquid splashes down on my pages. I snap my gaze up, looking to see who spilled a drink on my book. I find my face an inch away from the most fantastic set of breasts I've seen in ages.

The soft, rounded globes nearly press against my nose

as their owner leans past me to hand drinks to customers who, I realize, are pressing against me from behind. I glance around and the line at the bar is at least three deep. The bartender doesn't seem frazzled, though. She and her rack move methodically, stretching and leaning to pour drinks, handing them to the waiting customers. Her fingers fly over the buttons on the register without her needing to look and she stuffs cash tips into the pitcher behind the bar as she mixes up soda with cheap liquor.

I decide not to say anything about a little ginger ale splashing on my book. I sip at the soda and stare at her, mesmerized. She's got curves for days—round hips in tight jeans, a gently rounded stomach beneath the previously-noticed incredible chest, which is highlighted by a tight black tank. I recognize her, but she looks different today somehow.

I don't go out much, but when I do, my family drags me to this place, and there isn't much turnover with the staff. All the athletes tip really well in exchange for adjusted drink strength as needed: strong when we're winning. Light on the liquor pours when we're losing. The staff here takes good care of all of us and, more than once, has distracted annoying fans who get a little too personal. I should remember her.

She catches me staring and winks at me as she pulls on two taps at once, perfectly pouring a pair of beers she then serves to another wave of patrons. I could watch her all night, but I realize that's creepy.

I try to focus on my book ... but I already know the ending of that story. Cara is doing amazing. The US office got all new management, and every soccer team in the country, from the pro level down to the tiniest kid league, received new training and funds to support players of all genders.

What I don't know is this bartender's name, her story, or whether she'd ever consider letting me get a closer look at her incredible body.

Eventually, the crowd at the bar starts to thin a bit, and I manage to read an entire page of my book since she's out of sight. But then I feel her presence across the wood from me, and she leans forward, her hair blocking the light so I can't read. I look up to meet her gaze.

"Can I ask you something?"

I blink at her, unable to think of anything smart to say in return. You know, like "sure" or "of course..." *Words, Wyatt. Come on, man...*

Eventually, she puts me out of my misery, refilling my soda with barely a glance. "Why are you sitting alone at a bar, reading a book, on New Year's Eve?"

CHAPTER 2
FERN

"HE'S HERE AGAIN. Hot and bookish." My best friend, Thora, pinches my butt as I tie my apron snugly around my waist. I yelp and swat at her as she grins, tying her apron in place.

The two of us have been working together for years. Thora's mom gets us a lot of gigs working the bars at the various professional sports stadiums around Pittsburgh, but tonight is the Holy Grail of lucrative shift work: New Year's Eve at Fuel Up, a popular bar near campus. It's also my final shift, since I'm starting a new job this semester and can't commit to a regular bar schedule.

I pull my cheat sheet from my pocket one more time, looking over the cocktail specials. A lot of them are standard drinks with Pittsburgh-themed names: Molten Iron for a rum and Coke, Neville Island Iced Tea instead of Long Island...that sort of thing. "I'm ready," I tell her, flexing my fingers.

"You better be ready for a fat tip." Thora makes suggestive gestures and elbows me as I try to ignore the subject of my infatuation. He comes in every few weeks and sits alone at the bar with a soda and a book, looking dark, sexy, and silently responsible.

I stomp on her foot with my Converse sneaker, and she yelps. "Will you knock it off with the tip talk? I already agreed it is going to happen. Don't make it weird."

Thora is one of the few people who knows that all my hard work academically and financially has meant there's a certain gap in my life experience. Namely, I've never had p-in-the-v sex. Like a lot of teen girls, I initially wanted it to be with someone special, and I spent all of high school working my ass off for a college scholarship, which meant that someone special never fit into my schedule.

Then, it just all felt weird and awkward, and starting last year, I told Thora I'd settle for someone half as talented as my vibrator. But – I recognize a pattern here: – I wasn't willing to slow down my studies and fellowship applications to go out in search of anyone's tip.

So here I am, on New Year's Eve, in my senior year of college. All my paperwork has been submitted for all the things, and I have an incredible work-study position for the spring term. I told Thora I wanted to leave workaholic, sexless Fern behind and usher in the new year as a woman who enjoys herself every now and again.

It was Thora's idea to go for Mr. Designated Driver's big D. She guessed correctly that he'd be here tonight, ready to safely usher his friends home. Unless... I can convince him to take me home instead. Thora raises a brow at me as she serves a pitcher of beer to a crowd of muscular student-athletes.

My target is oblivious to it all, periodically flicking a long finger to turn the page of tonight's book. I lean forward on the bar, clasping my hands in front of my chest as I stretch to see if I can read the book title. Something about a Beautiful Game. I lick my lips and straighten my ponytail. "Can I ask you something?" He looks up at me, and his mouth opens and closes a few times. I probably startled him, so I just plow ahead. "Why are you sitting alone at a bar, reading a book, on New Year's Eve?"

His brow shoots up under the brim of his hat. "I hate crowds. I like reading." He shrugs.

I laugh. "Why not snuggle up on your couch with that book, then?"

And then he shoots me a real smile, a cocky grin that tips to one side before he licks his lips and closes the book. "Maybe I like having someone refill my drink while I read."

I pull out the nozzle and press the button to fire some more ginger ale into his glass. He laughs and watches me as I reach for a cherry to plop in. It's symbolic, although he doesn't know that.

I point to the book. "So, you're a soccer fan, then?"

He laughs again. "You could say that." He slides the book into his lap. "What about you? More of a hockey fan?"

I shrug. "I mostly think about juggling flaming bottles while mixing drinks. You know, really wow the crowds." A customer waves his hand, and I hold up a finger to the bookworm while I pour the guy a pair of cheap beers.

I catch my stranger's eye again and make my way back to him. He leans forward. "You're ambitious. I like it. But seriously, what are you into?"

I bite my lip and lean toward him. We're almost touching, and I can smell the ginger ale on his breath. I have to shout over the roar of the bar. "Honestly? I'm just trying to finish my degree and get out of here."

He nods, his eyes serious. "I can respect that. I'm right there with you."

I stare into his dark eyes, and I think my panties really do melt a little. "I'm Fern," I tell him, extending a hand.

"Wyatt." He gives me a shake, his hand warm despite the ice in the glass he's been clutching. "Wyatt Moyer."

The bar is three-deep with rowdy bodies, the jukebox is blaring, and I'm sort of just dumping various liquids into glasses and hoping for the best. I really can't ignore my work to talk to this guy, but now I know his name is Wyatt, and his palm is callused.

A customer waves a hand in front of my eyes to get my attention and Wyatt frowns, but I hold up an index finger again and wait on the newcomer. He leaves a soggy five on the bar, and I shove it into the tightly packed tip jar. My mouth waters, thinking about what I can do with that money. A new laptop, for starters, capable of running Python and saving my work. But if I get accepted into my dream fellowship in the U.K., I'll also need a ton of professional clothes, a student visa, the works.

I pour a few Molten Irons, envisioning the day I can actually afford my plane ticket across the pond. When I glance back at Wyatt, he's reading again. I keep one eye on him as I serve a round of beers mixed with a few pitchers of the spiked iced tea. I give a heavy pour on the rum, observing Wyatt's fingers turning the page gently, like he's worried he'll rip the paper. I watch as he uses his left index finger to smooth down the center of the book, pressing the spine open in a way that only seems lewd to me because I'm sex-starved. Surely.

There's a brief lull in the demand for drinks, and Thora catches me staring. She waggles her eyebrows, and I shrug. He's got a hint of dark stubble on his sharp jaw and full lips that tip up and down, moving between a frown and a small smile as he reads. His hand absently spins the soda glass, and I look my fill at his long fingers, the tendons in his hands practically dancing as he moves the cup.

It's now or never. There's only about two hours before midnight. Technically, I can leave whenever I want. I know Thora will keep my tips safe if I split before we close. I take a deep breath and grip the edge of the bar, standing in front of Wyatt. He puts the book down and looks up at me, smiling.

Emboldened by his warm facial expression, I charge ahead. "Any interest in me pouring drinks at your place? While you read … or whatever?"

Wyatt rubs a hand on his chin, considering. I'm not great at this, but I sense a look of combined surprise and desire on his face. He's quiet for a long time, long enough that I worry I blew it and ruined everything. Oh, god, what if he's gay? Or taken? As if he can read the panic on my face, he blows out a breath. "You're gorgeous, Fern. But are you sure? There's a lot of guys here who can maybe …" He looks around like he's trying to decide what a guy should be able to do for me.

I place a hand on his and meet his eye, drawing on confidence I had no idea lurked inside me. Desperate times, I guess. "Wyatt, I don't want a guy who can do anything other than get me off. I don't have time for more than that."

He takes a sip of his drink, chewing one of the ice cubes in his glass. I reach past his fingers and pluck the cherry back from his soda, biting it from the stem and hoping I don't look like an idiot. He leans back in his bar chair and I'm pretty sure he adjusts himself before he crosses his arms and squints at me. "Did my cousin put you up to this?"

"What? No. I don't know you. How would I know your cousin?"

Wyatt bites his lip and looks behind him, evidently spotting the cousin in question among the crowd of rowdy, laughing athlete guys. Wyatt pulls off his hat and rubs at his hair, which is a little long on top but shaved on the sides and back. Suddenly, all I want to do is run my hands through it, learn the shape of his haircut, and feel those sweaty strands between my fingers. He's hot. I look pretty good. This has to happen, right?

Wyatt nods, like he's finished having a similar internal monologue. "Your place or mine?"

I rip the apron off my waist and make eye contact with Thora, who claps a hand over her mouth and jumps up and down and makes the okay sign with her other hand. "Yours. I have to leave here through the back door. Meet me in the alley?"

CHAPTER 3
WYATT

ON ONE HAND, this alley is pretty private, and I feel a sense of calm knowing nobody is going to run up to me to ask about my season, my prospects, or my parents.

On the other, it's dark as hell and I hate that Fern was going to head out here alone in the middle of the night. I lean against the warm brick wall, waiting anxiously for her to emerge, questioning my decisions. What am I even doing, bringing a woman home for a one-night stand?

I've had teammates do this and wake up to find pictures of their ass plastered across social media. Something in my gut tells me Fern isn't going to do that. I get the feeling she's all business, all the time. And for some reason, she decided tonight her business is me.

The door opens with a burst of light and loud noise, and Fern slips into the alley, shivering a bit in her coat. I catch a brief look of hesitation on her face, but then she smiles and approaches me. "So, where do you live?"

I extend an arm for her to walk ahead of me down the alley and toward Forbes Avenue and my stellar parking spot. "I'm just a few blocks away, but my cousins made me drive." I glance at her and unlock the Rover. "Heated seats!"

Her eyes widen, seeing the car. I sort of like that she doesn't seem to know who I am. She clearly wasn't expecting a nice car like this. "Wow." She climbs inside and runs her hands along the leather arm rest. I close her door and walk around to my side, climbing in and turning on the engine as Fern massages my interior. Our hands brush when I reach for the gear shift, and I feel a jolt of electricity running through my body that has nothing to do with the V-8.

I clear my throat and flick on the button to warm Fern's seat. She smiles and settles in. "Wow. That heated up so fast. Okay, I'm never leaving this car."

I turn around to check behind me as I back out of the parking spot, catching her staring at me when I pull onto the busy three-lane street. "So, you'll be serving me sodas from the passenger seat?"

I sort of like cracking jokes with her. I relax into the idea of getting naked with this woman, getting up close and personal with her incredible curves. But when I glance her way, she seems tense, so I reach for her hand, running a thumb across her knuckles. "Just 'til graduation," she clarifies. "After that, I'll move out."

"Upgrade to an RV?" I turn through Schenley Park so I can loop back around to Atwood Street. Out of habit I give a wave to the dinosaur statue, feeling a bit dumb. My parents often took me and my sister to the history museum and joked about the dinosaurs playing soccer with their eggs.

Fern sighs. "Hopefully, I'll upgrade to a lorry. Or whatever counts as a luxury vehicle in England."

I nod. "I'm trying to move abroad myself. Do you have a job lined up?"

She shakes her head and closes her eyes, continuing to rub her palms along the now-warm seat. "I applied for a few fellowships. If it all goes to plan, I'll live in a van by the river Thames and get a PhD."

There are no spots near our apartment, of course, and I grit my teeth as I prepare to circle the block and look for parking. "You might be better off with an apartment you can walk to and from."

Fern sits up straighter. "Didn't you say you were your cousins' ride? How will they get home?"

I growl in frustration, turning onto a street two blocks from my door. "They'll have less of a walk than us now that all the parking is gone. I should have made them hoof it, to begin with."

Fern points to a spot on the left side of the street. "There's one!"

I nod and parallel-park while she stares at me again. Maybe I back up an extra time, just to be sure. I grin and unbuckle, turning to face her. "If you can stand the walk, I have the heat on in my apartment. No leather, but the couch isn't too bad."

Fern opens her door, catching me off guard. I run around the side of the car in time to at least close it for her. She smiles. There's heat in her gaze, and I take her hand, making our way down the street. She looks up at me, blowing her dark hair from her eyes. "You never said why you're leaving the country. Grad school?"

I shake my head, incredulous. She has no idea. This is amazing. "I've got some job prospects in Mexico." A half-truth, a small omission. I can be anybody I want tonight. I can be Wyatt Moyer for real, with a woman who hasn't memorized my stats or searched the internet for my parents, or bookmarked news stories from when my bio dad was arrested for leaving me in a hot car while he went into a bar.

"This is me," I say, fishing in my pocket for my keys and unlocking the outer door to the building.

"I thought these apartments were all for athletes..." Fern looks around, then her eyes widen, and she claps a hand over her mouth. "Oh, duh. You came in with all the athlete guys." She squeezes my arm like she's checking for muscles. I'm happy to have her find them. "What sport are you? Swimmer?"

I laugh. "Hardly. No, I play soccer." I tilt my head toward my apartment door and move to unlock it.

Fern follows me, babbling. "I should have known. Your book had a soccer ball on the cover. Sometimes, I'm so deep in my own business that I just don't notice other people's details. Which is probably a sign I wasn't meant to be a bartender long-term."

I set the book in question on the counter, along with my keys, while Fern looks around—I'm assuming for someplace to hang her coat. I'm not even sure what the most gentlemanly protocol is here. I'd grab her and kiss her right now, but that seems kind of overkill. I swallow but decide to just tell her, "You can put your stuff in my room if you want."

I gesture down the hall to the open door where my cousins gave me crap a few hours earlier. She nods and heads in there. I follow, snapping on the light to reveal a space I'm pretty glad I keep neat. She takes in my king-sized bed with a black duvet, a dresser full of athletic clothes, and a small desk with a lamp and laptop. She notices the bookshelf and touches the books, smiling at the rows of cracked spines. I've always been a reader—lots of time on buses to and from away games.

Fern sets her coat on my desk with a clunk, and I figure she has all her stuff in her pockets since she doesn't have a purse. My sister always has a huge purse that could double as a duffel bag.

I clear my throat. "I, uh, don't do this very often."

Fern bites her lip and nods. "Me neither."

"We don't have to do anything." I scratch the back of my neck and pull off my hat, tossing it on the desk on top of her coat. "I'm happy to keep reading my book while you bring me San Pellegrino."

Fern tosses her head back and guffaws. "God, even your soda is fancy." She takes a step toward me and runs a finger from my shoulder to my elbow. I twitch under her touch, feeling ticklish and electrified. "I didn't come here to pour drinks."

"Good." I lean forward and press my lips against hers.

CHAPTER 4
FERN

MAN, this feels good. Wyatt wraps his arms around me, hands splayed across my back and butt as he kisses me. His lips are just as soft as they looked, and I love the feel of them pressed against mine. I can feel the warmth of his body, the delicious strength of him, and a moan escapes my throat as we kiss.

Kissing, just seeking pleasure for the sake of it, is so foreign to me. I'm so used to working hard toward specific goals. It's delicious, just standing here with my arms around him, exploring his mouth.

He seems to enjoy the sounds I'm making and releases his own deep moan. I pull back with a gasp, not expecting the vibrations that buzz through his chest at his sounds. Wyatt smiles at me wolfishly and then leans back in, biting my lower lip as he backs me up to the edge of his bed.

I sink onto the mattress, and he stands between my legs, running his hands through my hair, gazing down at me like I'm made of some precious material he doesn't want to hurt. "Just checking in with you, Fern. Are you comfortable with this?"

I nod. He nods back, finger tracing my cheek. "Good, beautiful, because I'm ready to give you a happy new year."

I start to laugh because it's an adorably dorky thing to say, but then he sinks to his knees and presses a hand to my sternum. I'm flat on my back on the bed as he lifts the hem of my shirt. "God, your body is incredible," he murmurs, planting kisses along the stomach I usually try to hide behind flowy or ruched tops. I don't even have time to feel self-conscious about it because Wyatt licks and nips his way along my ribcage.

I move to take off my tank and while he watches, literally licking his lips. "Fern, I've been hard for you since the moment you pressed your chest in my face at the bar." Wyatt seems surprised by the confession but also seems to recover quickly at the sight of my too-big boobs spilling out of last year's bra. "Holy shit, look at you."

I glance down to see what he sees, but my view is blocked by his head as Wyatt yanks off the bra and presses his mouth to my nipple. The wet heat of his tongue has me gasping, prickles of pleasure zooming through my body as he kneads and squeezes and licks, moaning and whispering praise the entire time. Why have I not made time for this sooner?

I place one hand on his shoulder, loving the subtle movements beneath his shirt. The more Wyatt suckles at me, pinching and teasing, the more I squirm beneath the weight of his torso. I realize he's working his way to the floor between my legs, and I crave pressure and friction against my center, but I can't quite get it in this position. I grunt in frustration and Wyatt looks up from his work.

He draws one finger down the center of my body, teasing at my crotch. The denim of my jeans is too thick, and I need more. "God," I curse, but I don't know what to say next. Do I just … demand that he touch me?

"You need it bad, don't you Fern?"

"Yes. Thank you. Please." I don't even know what I'm saying, but he laughs, and I feel his long fingers unbuttoning my pants. Before I can form any sort of response, my legs are in the air, my jeans and panties are ripped off, and my thighs are smooshed against Wyatt's ears while his hands press the soft, sensitive skin of my upper legs closer to his head, like he's trying to drown himself in my body.

And then he spreads me open and studies me, like I'm a page in one of his books–intently, like there's nothing else in the room.

"Oh, I wasn't expecting … oh, wow." I raise myself up on my forearms just in time to see Wyatt Moyer stare at my vulva like it's the most incredible thing he ever laid eyes on. And then, with a sigh, he leans forward and licks me there. "Wyatt!" He freezes and looks up, eyes questioning. "I'm all … sweaty. I was just working for hours."

"And?"

I bite my lip. "And, doesn't it smell?"

He sniffs, and my cheeks heat. But he's not turning away in disgust. He looks like he is about to have a stroke from pleasure, somehow. "It smells like a pussy, Fern."

"Okay, but … you like that?"

He dips a finger inside me gently, and I suck in a breath. I bear down on him involuntarily, arching my back to see if I can get any friction where I need it on my clit. "I like it a lot, yeah. It smells like you're turned on, and I really like that."

Well, I can't argue with him. If I hadn't been turned on before, the sight of him staring at my body with hooded eyes, blown pupils, and reverence would have me dripping all over his sheets. Who am I to deny him something he apparently likes, right? Right? Maybe if I had more experience, I wouldn't feel so vulnerable. Before I can protest again, Wyatt licks me again, slowly, his tongue flat and wide, and deliciously warm. "Oh, wow. Okay. Yes. Ohhhhhh wow."

Wyatt licks and thrusts his finger in and out. His hands are somehow everywhere on my body, all at once. I feel his fingers on my thighs, my nipples, my folds. I feel his tongue lapping and pressing until I'm a coiled spring of need. I realize my legs are pressed hard against his head, smothering him perhaps, but I am powerless to do anything but fist the sheets. I moan as he licks and glides and sucks until I'm tipping over the edge. Electric shudders roll through my body, lifting me up and out of my consciousness. I think I'm shouting his name. I think I'm squeezing my legs together in time with my waves of pleasure.

I drop a hand lazily to my stomach, and my eyes drift close. I stop moaning, switching over to a gentle hum as I enjoy the small aftershocks rumbling through my body. When I open my eyes, Wyatt is standing in front of me shirtless, dropping his jeans, palming the bulge in his boxer briefs with one hand as he wipes his mouth with the back of his other. I blurt, "Jesus. You look filthy. Like sexy-filthy. Sorry." I move to sit up, but Wyatt shakes his head, crawling over me like some sort of jungle cat predator.

"I am filthy, Fern." I scoot up the bed 'til I'm near the pillow, and he bows down, giving me his weight and kissing me, and wow. I definitely taste myself on his lips. My eyes widen in shock. One corer of his mouth hooks up in a grin. "What?" When I can't say anything, he smiles.

"Hasn't anyone ever done that for you before? Made you come with their mouth?"

I shake my head, and his smile widens. "They've been missing out. You taste incredible."

Before I can ask him if he really means that, he juts his hips against mine, and I feel the thick rod of his erection. Is he hard like that for me? From getting me off? My blood fizzes at the thought that he enjoyed smashing his face in my sweaty snatch, especially as he starts groaning again, pressing his big hands into my boobs. "These feel so incredible. So soft. Your body is like a dream, Fern."

Wyatt rocks his hips against mine while he praises me, and I wrap my ankles around his knees, knowing I'm so wet that I'm getting his underwear damp. "Take these off," I tell him, like I know what I'm doing, and I start sliding the cotton over the swell of his ass and holy shit.

He wriggles out of his boxer briefs, and I look over his shoulder to see the most amazing backside. It has dips in the sides where the taut muscles of his legs meet those solid glutes. I press my palms into the dips, my fingers digging into his cheeks, and wow, I can feel the whole rigid length of him rubbing against my heat.

I tuck my chin and adjust myself on the bed because I want to see it between us, want to know what an erect cock looks like in person, and it's better than I imagined. Wyatt's shaft is long and darker than the skin of his butt. The uncut tip glistens with a bead of moisture, and I can't tell whether it came from me or him. I reach for it, amazed at how warm and smooth it feels in my hand, yet also impossibly hard. I rub the liquid on the tip with my thumb, spreading the fluid around the shiny head as he nibbles my ear and squeezes my boobs. Everything feels so good, so much, so amazing.

Wyatt rolls to one side, and I see him fumbling around the drawer of his nightstand . He pinches a foil packet between his fingers and moves to tear it open. I sit up. "Can I do it?" I am overcome with a burning desire to be the one to roll the condom onto him, to feel it snugly in place before he slides inside me. I'm not worried about pain, somehow. I've used toys in the past ... a lot, of late. And I know my body is soft after he made me come that hard.

I'm throbbing with anticipation, with the need to have this part of him inside of me.

Wyatt stares in silent wonder as I take my time lining up the condom, rolling it down him slowly. When I glance up to meet his eye, we smile at one another like we just achieved something together. I have a moment of concern that I don't know what he likes, but then he asks, "You ready, Fern?" Wyatt runs a finger along my jaw again. I realize he already has things he does that turn me on. And he seems to like my enjoyment.

"Yes, please." I lie back down, settling onto the pillow and tipping my thighs open as he crawls back between them. Wyatt keeps his gaze locked on mine and uses his hand to line himself up, and then ... it's happening. I feel him sliding inside, a burst of fullness followed by a pinch and then exquisite satisfaction.

CHAPTER 5
WYATT

I FREEZE when I'm inside Fern, overwhelmed by the sensation and intensity of our connection. I stare down at her with my weight on my hands. She winces briefly but then seems to love what she's experiencing because I can feel her pulsing around me, drawing me in deeper. "Oh, yes, Wyatt. Please. Yes."

Fuck, this woman is so damn hot. She's like a creamy, delicious dessert, all curves and softness, wrapped entirely around me with her arms, legs, and velvety pussy. I could drown here, happily, enveloped in the tangy sweat of her. My sheets are going to smell like this for days, and I'm going to fall asleep achingly hard at the memory of how this feels right now.

I let her have a little more of my weight, and I think she likes that because she pulls me tighter against her torso. And then Fern starts moving beneath me, rolling her hips, muttering my name, spewing profanity. "Do you need to come again, beautiful? Is that what's wrong?"

I grin at her as her eyes fly wide, and she nods. "Yes. Please?"

"You don't need to beg me, Fern. Fuck, you feel good." I adjust my weight so I can touch her, reaching between us to press a thumb into her clit. She's so damn responsive. I can tell immediately when she likes something, which gives me so many clues about when she doesn't. It doesn't take me long to find the pressure and rhythm she needs to go wild. "You're making me lose my damn mind, Fern."

She seems beyond speech, thrashing beneath me. At one point, she sinks her teeth into my shoulder, and I can feel her coming, pulsing and squeezing around me. I can't hold back anymore. I put all my weight on my forearms and start rolling my hips with full intensity, driving her into the mattress, grunting like an animal until I feel the ball of white-hot pleasure building at the base of my spine.

Fern reaches between my legs and squeezes my balls, her expression pure sex. The feel of her, and the look of her, and the sound of my name on her lips sends me over the edge. I'm coming into the condom, pulsing inside her as I press my forehead into hers until I'm totally spent.

———

My chest heaves as I try to calm down. Fern traces a lazy hand through the hair on the leg I have bent up over her hip. I press a kiss to her forehead and her eyes fly open, almost like she forgot I was here. I smile down at her, wanting to stroke her hair and hold her tight. Which is insane because I never want to do those things. We just had a one-night stand. I should be itching to get her out of here so I can shower. "Hey," I say.

"Um, hey." She bites her lip and looks around. "I … should probably go."

"I'm still inside you," I point out, although I slide out

when she shifts to sit up. I reach for her hand. "If you give me twenty minutes, we can do an encore."

Fern huffs out a laugh. "Twenty minutes, huh? That's the recovery period?"

I shrug and kiss her cheek. "Don't go anywhere."

I dash into the en suite bathroom to deal with the condom. I realize I don't have a washcloth , so I take a hand towel and run it under the hot water. When I get back to the bedroom, Fern has already put on her bra and her tank top, and she's looking around the room like she's searching for the bottom half of her clothes. "Hey," I tell her. "Lie back and let me take care of you a minute at least."

Her eyes widen and I gesture with the towel. She settles back onto the bed, looking down as I gently rub the towel between her legs, kissing her inner thighs. As I get closer to her pussy, she tenses. "Sore?"

She nods. "Just a little. It was totally worth it, though. I didn't mean—"

I grin. "It's okay." I dab at her gently with the wash cloth. "We don't have to do another round, but you definitely aren't walking home in the middle of the night."

"Oh, I wasn't going to walk. I live in Brookline…"

I scoff. "Isn't that at least two buses away? On New Year's Eve?"

She shrugs, and I toss the towel into the bathroom. At least it lands on the tile floor. I climb into the bed and try to tuck Fern against my side, running my hands through her hair until I feel her body ease up a bit. "It's one bus and one train." Her words are slow, sleepy.

"I'll drive you in the morning. Stay."

Fern sighs and wriggles against me, her bottom half is

still naked. I wrap an arm around her, naked myself, and rest my palm on her butt. This is perfection.

———

When I wake up a few hours later, in the gray light of early dawn on a new year, I'm alone in my bed. No note, no Fern, no way to contact her for a repeat.

I sigh and drape an arm across my face as I hear Odin getting ready for the combine. It's probably just as well. I wasn't lying when I told her I couldn't commit to anything more than casual. If everything goes to plan, I'll be moving in a few months.

CHAPTER 6
FERN

THORA

You ready to slay the day? [vampire emoji]

ME

Is that really the right image for that text?

THORA

I couldn't find a wooden stake emoji

ME

What, no Buffy GIF?

THORA

So, I take it you're not nervous. Now that you've propositioned a hottie, you're ready for anything!

———

I HADN'T TAKEN the time to consider my night with Wyatt last week as any sort of bravery benchmark. I guess my friend is right, though. I sort of proved to myself that it's okay to ask for what I want and trust myself in new situations. New Year's Eve worked out pretty damn well, after all.

But on the other hand, I'm not nervous about teaching because it's basic algebra, and I am pretty confident I'm good at explaining those concepts to other people.

I put on my "teaching outfit" that Thora helped me pick out: brand-new-used designer jeans from the thrift store south of the city, a bright yellow blazer from the same store, and a cute striped shirt I already had. Thora and I have been trying to build capsule wardrobes to mix and match professional pieces for when we start graduate school, and need to look less like bartenders.

I don't want my students to think of me as "that chick who always wears the yellow blazer." But some things are too good to pass by, even when funds are tight. Veronica Beard new with tags for seven dollars ? That's just good sense.

I take an early train downtown and smile as I blend in with the other commuters, transferring to a bus heading toward campus. Undergrads don't usually get the chance to be teaching assistants for recitations, but there are way more first-year math students than usual and fewer grad students to cover the classes this spring.

My mentor, Professor Yoon, suggested I submit an application. I'm pretty sure they just needed that as a formality, but I'm grateful for the experience ... and the money. I thought there would maybe be some more training or that I could meet some of the grad students who are also leading recitation, but they are basically throwing me in with the wolves.

They lecture twice a week in a huge auditorium, and then the third class of the week is broken up into twenty-student groups where we TAs answer students' questions and reinforce the material. Dr. Yoon sent out the syllabus to all of us, their admin let us know where there were cubicles we could use for office hours, and someone from the math department made sure I had a copy of the textbook. And that was it. No fanfare, but I guess they wouldn't have picked me for this gig if they didn't know I'm responsible.

I'm really looking forward to this, rather than feeling nervous. I like explaining things to other people. I like it when they ask me questions because seeing what others are confused by is a really interesting way for me to rethink the concepts. And I'm not in charge of the curriculum—just making sure the students grasp the material Dr. Yoon lays out.

Recitation is graded pass/fail based entirely on attendance, so I don't even have to worry about anyone getting mad at me over grades. I have my roster printed in a folder full of notes and a ton of extra copies of the syllabus. I did look over the names and there are a handful of older students. I'm assuming they couldn't fit the required math class into their schedule until now. Or maybe they forgot they had to take it to graduate. Or maybe they're just bad at math. For now!

I have daydreams of convincing them all that the language of the universe can be applied everywhere. I know they won't all leave here in love with algebra, but I know I can help them understand how to approach these concepts and how to succeed in this class.

I arrive at the towering building, with students streaming in and out of the revolving doors. I hold my head high as I type 23 on the elevator call box, and soon, I'm zooming up to one of the newer classrooms, full of projectors, whiteboards, and everything I need to write out complex equations larger than life.

I write my name on the board with ALGEBRA 1 RECITATION.

I spread my things on the podium at the front of the room but then decide I'd rather we all sit in a circle, so I pick a desk for my stuff and arrange the other chairs in a ring so we're all facing each other—or we will be once the students start showing up.

I slide into my seat and run my finger along my printed roster. I come across a student named Wyatt DeLuca. My cheeks heat, remembering my night with a different Wyatt.

Thora was right. Sex is a huge stress reliever. I couldn't walk properly for a day and a half after my night with Wyatt Moyer, but I took a hot bath, touched myself thinking of how I got that sore and went into this first week of class of my final semester of college feeling more relaxed than ever.

I shake these thoughts away as the first groups of students trickle in. I smile at them. "Hey, I'm Fern. Sit anywhere you like!" They do, mostly ignoring me and one another as they check their phones or work on the cross-word from the student paper. I check my watch, and it's exactly ten, so I get up and walk toward the door to close it just as the last straggling students slip in.

I stumble when I see Wyatt—my Wyatt—duck into the room with a muttered apology. I back up toward my desk, hitting it and knocking my folder to the ground in a flutter of papers. He crouches to pick up the pile of syllabi, and his eyes meet mine as he hands them to me. I freeze in horror as I realize he's a student in this class. Why the hell would he lie about his name?

CHAPTER 7
WYATT

"MOM, I have to go. I'm late for class." She always calls at the worst times. I lean against the wall and close my eyes, knowing my mother means well but also wishing she'd butt out just a little. Most parents aren't intimately familiar with the process of getting signed to a professional sports team. Lucky me, both my mom and my stepdad coach professional sports teams.

I am lucky. I have amazing parents. I mutter this to myself as Mom keeps on offering pointers.

"You really should touch base with Brian. I can have Dad talk to him if you want. We'd love you to stay here in Pittsburgh. Imagine if you could play for your dad? Wouldn't that be so fun?" My stepdad, Hawk Moyer, is the only real father I've ever known. He embodies that role so completely it's hard for me to remember that I have a biological father…and I never use that word in reference to Nick.

I pinch the bridge of my nose. "Like I told you, Brian is talking to teams in Mexico. I'm really focused on finishing my degree right now, Mom. And I'm going to be late for the math class I should have taken four years ago."

She hums. "Okay, honey. I just love you so much, and I'm so proud of you." Her voice catches. "You've overcome so much."

"I love you, too, Mom." I see the last group of students walk into the classroom I'm supposed to join. The teacher, presumably, comes to the door to close it. "Gotta go, bye."

I hang up on my mom and jog to the door just as it's closing, and in my haste, I bump into the teacher's desk, sending a pile of papers fluttering to the ground. I worry I hurt her or something because she stiffens and doesn't move to pick anything up. I tug my hat lower on my head and crouch. I really wanted to get here early to remind the professor they're not supposed to say my name during roll call.

For one thing, I hate when other students in class identify me as "that soccer player." They don't know anything about me except that I'm good at sports. I wish there were a way to just … be a professional athlete and not talk to fans. All the press conferences and fan fests just remind me of being in custody court. My parents are always talking to reporters. I should be used to the recognition, but it all makes my skin crawl.

I gather the last of the papers and look up to hand them to the professor. Except it's not a professor. It's Fern. From the other night.

Her eyes are wide, and she stands frozen in the middle of the classroom. I look around and see ALGEBRA 1 RECITATION written on the board … along with Fern's name. Shit.

"Are you my professor?"

The question seems to snap her out of her shock, and

she snatches the pile of papers from my hand. She strides over to her seat and clears her throat. I take this as my cue to pour myself into a desk. I was hoping to hide in the back, but she has all the chairs arranged in a circle so everyone can see everyone else. Great.

"I'm Fern and I'm the TA for this recitation," she says in a thin voice so unlike her confident bartender voice or even the voice she used in my bedroom. I cannot let myself think about her in the bedroom, especially if she really is my teacher. I tug on my hat again. I need to face the fact that she is in charge of my grade for this course.

I fucked my professor.

Fern takes a deep breath and holds up a piece of paper. "I passed the syllabus around, so you should each take one of those and look it over. I know it's weird that the semester started on a Thursday, and you're having recitation before you even meet Dr. Yoon. They will lecture on Mondays and Wednesdays. And of course, we meet on Fridays." She laughs a little nervously, and some of the other students join in, but most don't, and Fern's cheeks turn a little pink.

I've heard her make better jokes. "Anyway, today we're just going to review the schedule, and if there's time, I can preview the topics for next week's lectures."

She summarizes the syllabus, and students around me highlight the dates for the exams, which Fern will help administer but not be grading. "Oh, speaking of grades," she pulls out a folder. "Recitation is one credit, and that's entirely based on attendance. Everyone gets two absences, no questions asked, but after that ..." She points to the syllabus, where I can see that there's a basic rubric for how many points off we get for being late or absent. "So, I guess I should take roll." Fern starts reading out names, and the students around me grunt or wave in response.

My heart starts racing. Students look around, eyeing each other up and looking for recognition as the names are read. It's only a matter of minutes until they recognize me from billboards and last year's college soccer video game. I need to head this shit off at the pass. I blurt, "I'm Wyatt. I'm here."

I can tell by Fern's face that they have me on the roster under my legal name toward the beginning of the alphabet. "Wyatt," I repeat as everyone stares. "I'm probably the only one on the roster." I gesture at Fern's list, and she nods, moving her pencil. She continues on through the roster as people murmur.

It's already too late. People recognize me. I hear someone ask their friend if they heard I got a shoe deal. I wish. Except, not really, because that would be a lot of fucking publicity. I just need to buy myself some time to get signed. I can focus on endorsements and all that super-star crap later. I just need to seal my first deal and get myself established, hopefully far away from American soil, where nobody knows anything about me from before I got good at soccer.

By the time my heart slows, and I can concentrate, the students around me are packing up and filing out. I kill time reading a book until the room clears out, and it's just me and Fern.

"Wyatt, may I speak to you?" Fern's voice is oddly formal, and I nod, staying in my seat until everyone leaves. I'm definitely not having any sort of conversation in front of other undergrads. Fern seems to expect our convo to start immediately, and she sighs and shifts over to a seat next to me.

She smells great, floral and fresh. Her outfit is damn fine, too. I liked her in jeans and a tight tank top, but this look suits her a lot. She looks professional and confident. Or I assume she looked confident until she saw me and realized *she* fucked one of her students. I grin at that. Damn right, she did.

"Wyatt." Her tone is angry now. "Why did you lie to me?"

CHAPTER 8
FERN

WYATT BLOWS OUT A LONG BREATH, takes off his baseball hat, and then shoves it back on his head, covering his eyes. "I didn't lie." I point at the roster, about to yell at him for gaslighting me, but he holds up a hand. "Not exactly. I just didn't tell you everything. It's not like we traded life stories."

I bite my lip. He's right that we didn't give each other a ton of information. But we did share something pretty intense. Or maybe it was just intense for me because I never did that before? Maybe that's always how sex is…an overwhelming connection and feeling that this other person can see directly into my soul and fill me with unreal pleasure…

"Look." Wyatt grips the edge of the desk attached to his chair so hard his knuckles are white. "The last name on your roster isn't supposed to be public information." I furrow my brow, and he explains that he has an alias. "I can't stand any association with the man who sired me, but that's what was on my birth certificate. So, I don't use it unless I have to." He takes off his hat and fiddles with his hair, a nervous habit apparently. "I go by Wyatt Moyer wherever I can. My mom calls it a stage name, but that makes it feel even more like I'm not really part of the family." He fidgets in his seat, and I stare, not knowing what to say about all of this. "Look," he pleads, eyes huge and doing things to my insides. "I did try to go into the system and change it to Moyer. I also tried to change it at the damn social security office, but that's a whole freaking production involving court and lawyers and shit."

Something about this revelation tugs at my heart. Maybe it's the look in his partially hidden eyes…the obvious pain and frustration there. "You're trying to change your name?"

He nods. "It doesn't feel like mine. It's my birth father's name, and he's a piece of shit. I go by my family's name, Moyer, and I swear I didn't try to mislead you or something to get in your pants."

My cheeks heat, and I grimace. "Well, I guess it was me pushing the pants situation."

He leans forward and grins. "You didn't have to push too hard, Fern."

It's my turn to take a deep breath. I stare down at the roster on my desk. "Okay. Well. I'm assuming you're not able to switch to another recitation section?"

He shakes his head rapidly. "My schedule is nuts between conditioning and weight room, and I'm not even in season right now."

"Mm. Well, I also have an intense schedule trying to finish with a double major in math and computer science, so that leaves us stuck together in a teacher-student situation." I fidget with the pen on my desk, not meeting his eye. "We need to keep things professional. No more flirting and definitely no repeats of New Year's Eve."

When I finally look at him, he's giving me a filthy look, like he's remembering every second of our night together before I slinked away from his bed like a thief. "Wyatt, I'm serious. I absolutely need this experience on my CV and—"

"Yeah, yeah. I get it." He flinches, like he's also trying to convince himself. "You're my teacher. I will be on my best student behavior. You'll barely notice me."

He grabs his backpack and heads for the door, leaving me to doubt my ability to ever concentrate in his presence. Staring at his ass in his gray sweats doesn't help me with this mission. Not one bit.

———

I'm supposed to meet Thora in the library to debrief. Neither of us has any other classes on Fridays, but since we both live so far off campus, we usually hang out and study together until lunch. She spots me approaching and makes exaggerated winky faces, fanning herself. "Fern, you look smoking hot. If I were your student, I'd have trouble paying attention."

I sink into the seat opposite her at the table. "You have no idea." She furrows her brow and I slump forward, head on my hands. "The guy from the bar is one of my students." Thora is silent long enough that I pop my head up to make sure she hasn't left. Her mouth hangs open a bit, and she blinks a few times. "Did you hear what I said?"

She grins. "Oh, I heard. And I've read this book before."

"What do you mean?"

Thora rubs her palms together. "Forbidden love. Hot as

fuck student. Sexy-as-hell professor. I probably have ten of those in my e-reader right now." She rummages in her bag like she's going to show me her romance novel collection.

"I'm not going to read one of your steamy books right now, Thora. This is serious."

She waves a hand. "I know. But … is it serious? It's recitation, right? Graded based on if he shows up to class?"

I clench my whole body. "Yeah but coming to class could feel unsafe for him. Or uncomfortable. I might be making him uncomfortable."

Thora nods. "Yes, I can see how your overt sexual energy would be unsettling for a young student-athlete about to sign a pro soccer contract."

I frown at her. "He's going pro?"

Thora rolls her eyes at me. "Are you telling me you didn't even look him up online after he was inside your body? Hell, I looked him up the minute things calmed down at the bar. Oh! I have your tips." Thora reaches into her cavernous bag, rummaging around until she pulls out a bright pink envelope stuffed to the ripping point. "It's mostly ones, I think. Mine was."

I slide the money into a zippered pocket of my bag, pinching it between my thighs in case someone wandering past gets any ideas. Not that I really believe everyone is out to rob me. I just really need that money to end up in my savings account ASAP.

Thora runs her fingers through her hair and looks at me. "Fern, I get it. You know I get it. And honestly, you're both seniors. You're both clearly dedicated to your own thing. I think you're mature enough to ignore him for an hour a week while you plan your climb up the academic ladder."

I nod. She's probably right. The shock of seeing him today will wear off.

We try to get things done for a bit before I give up, too distracted by Wyatt and what could happen now that he's my student. "I need to go deposit those tips." I sigh. "And my mom will probably want to touch base about teaching anyway."

"You gonna tell her about Wyatt?"

I squint, considering. "It's not like I pour out my soul about guys and stuff like that ... how would I even bring it up?"

Thora shrugs. "Mama Montgomery is very reasonable. And she'll sniff you out in a heartbeat if you don't tell her something. Why not just say one of your students is a guy you were interested in last semester."

I nod, tapping my fingers on my bag full of precious, dangerous cargo. "It's not technically a lie..."

I stand up, checking the time on my phone. "All right. I'll talk to you later. You working this weekend?"

Thora nods. I wave to her and run outside in time to catch the bus downtown.

———

I have an entire hour on public transit to figure out what to tell my mom, so by the time I get to the bank where she works, I'm feeling much calmer about the whole situation.

Mom looks up from her teller window , smiling when she sees me. I slide the pink envelope across the counter. "I'd like to make a deposit, please!"

She glances at the envelope, still taped shut. "You didn't even use any of it to buy yourself something nice?"

I make a face. "Mom. What am I gonna get that's nice?"

She sighs. "We can do a treat every now and then, Fern Montgomery. It isn't sustainable to keep living like monks while you save and save for the next thing."

I grab a deposit slip and start filling it out. "I know, Mom. And I am easing up a little. I told you I went out with friends on New Year's Eve after my shift. And I'm not even working this weekend." I don't add that my only friend *is* working, so I'm still not doing anything social. "We should have a movie marathon."

Mom's face brightens. "We can get takeout. You can tell me all the latest news about your fellowship."

I slide her the completed deposit slip. Mom doesn't ask for my ID, but I show it to her anyway. I don't want anyone to be checking a video or something and get her in trouble. "There's nothing to tell right now until they make their decisions. You know that, Mom."

And she does know it. She was once a bright student like me, applying for scholarships and looking at colleges. She got pregnant with me and moved in with my dad, and they both made a real go at juggling school and parent-hood … until it got really hard, and Dad took off. He didn't go far physically, but he also never really seemed to mature much, and he's certainly never offered either of us any support, financially or emotionally.

Mom hands me a receipt for my deposit, and we both smile a bit at the balance number on my account. Slowly and steadily, I'm getting closer to my benchmarks. Assuming I get accepted into one of the programs … I can't let myself worry about what might happen if I don't. I say, "I'll make dinner tonight and queue up that new Reese Witherspoon movie for when you get home." I grin and squeeze Mom's hand. She squeezes back and waves me off.

CHAPTER 9
WYATT

"YOU'RE WYATT MOYER, right? From the soccer team?" A woman with bleached blond hair sits in the seat next to mine as I try to slip into the back of the recitation section the next week. I glance over at her. Any other year, I'd be into her glossy pink lips and the view of her lacy bra from the cut-off collar of the baggy sweatshirt she wears. Today, I just want to get through class without angering Fern.

I'm not in the best mood for superfans. My legs are aching from lifting weights with the team this morning. My fingers are cramped from texting my parents repeatedly that I haven't signed any contracts yet.

"Yeah," I grunt, keeping my eyes on my notebook and hoping my body language communicates that this isn't going to be a lead-up to a hookup.

She slides her chair closer to mine. "My roommates and I *love* soccer. We were there for your hat trick this fall. Against Maryland?"

I nod. "Yeah. Thanks for coming out." I hate this. If I'm going to play pro, I know I need to at least be nice to fans.

But honestly, it's all I can manage right now trying to figure out my professional life, stay in shape, and not pop a boner over the TA for this math recitation.

As I draw nonsense notes in my notebook, I see a hand with manicured nails slide a piece of paper onto my desk. I look up again and my fan is smiling at me. "That's my number. If you ever need to catch up on notes or whatever." She lifts her brows at me seductively. My mind reels, trying to figure out what I can say to politely let her know I won't be reaching out to her for homework help or anything else.

She's probably memorized every factoid about me online, and that always weirds me out.

I'm saved by Fern clapping her hands and shouting, "Okay, everyone, let's get down to reducing equations." She smiles and shakes her head. "That's sort of funny if you understand math concepts." She's adorable, making nerd jokes. Nobody laughs, of course, because it's ass-early on a Friday, and we're all here because we suck at math.

I try to sink low in my seat and stare at her, which is expected of students and teachers. Except I'm not looking at the right things. I'm not watching the numbers and letters she writes on the board—I'm staring at that lush ass and remembering how it felt to dig my fingers into her soft skin. When she lifts her arm to write on the board, I'm staring at her silhouette, wanting to palm her tits again, maybe while she whispers into my ear about finding square roots.

Fern was the absolute perfect distraction for me from all the pressures in my life, and now … I'm distracted by my distraction.

I'm so fucked. I wonder if I'd still be this into her if she wasn't my teacher. Would I go for a brainiac gal? I've never really sought anyone out for more than casual fun. I'm not entirely sure what I'm hoping for with Fern. Just a fantasy? A fucking amazing memory to use when I jerk off in the morning? A repeat, so I can carry around the knowledge that I boned my teacher?

She tosses the dry-erase marker on the shelf with a clatter and smiles at the board. "Does anyone else have a question about the substitution method?"

She looks around expectantly. Nobody moves or talks. I glance at my watch and see we're only about halfway through the session. I don't want her to have to stand up there while a room full of assholes makes her squirm. But I wasn't paying enough attention to what she was saying to come through and ask a question of my own.

Apparently, I don't need to worry about Fern, though, because she raises one eyebrow and crosses her arms, popping one hip out in a move I'm sure is unconscious but definitely communicates that she knows absolutely everything there is to know about whatever method she just mentioned. "Not one of you wants to know about using the distributive property? Hint: this will definitely be on the exam…"

Still, nobody talks. Fern circles the room once, and I can tell she's playing with us. She knows none of us have any idea what's going on, but everyone is paying attention now, leaning in as she talks. "Could it be that none of you remember what the distributive property actually is?" Fern laughs and returns to the board. "Let's break it down."

———

A half-hour later, everyone files out of the room. I can still feel the buzz in the air that comes when a bunch of people are all figuring something out together. Fern really is good at teaching this shit. I shove my notebook in my bag and try to slip out the back. I know if I look at her, I will betray something with my facial expression.

So, I'm not really paying attention when I leave the building, heading toward my apartment to grab some food before my afternoon classes. I pull out my phone to order takeout and see a series of texts from *him*.

> Can't avoid me forever, son.

I can picture my biological father, Nick, in my mind, glassy eyes looking dead inside. His muscles bulge like he's still hitting the gym for hours a day despite getting himself declared physically disabled and incapable of working — or paying a single cent of child support to my mother.

I hate that I reached out to him, that I brought this on. My hands shake as I scroll through the messages. The first time I reached out was to let him know I was changing my name. I had to file a notice in the newspaper. He was going to see it anyway. I figured we'd clear the air and move on, maybe get a beer sometime.

He immediately began demanding I send him money to make up for years of him being denied the right to be my father or something. I realized pretty quickly that I hadn't been catastrophizing any of those memories. This guy is a real piece of shit.

> Saw your name on a potential roster for the Olympics, kid. Be a shame if someone leaked dirt on your mother. Did I hear that she was accused of sexual misconduct?

I school my face to remain expressionless. The thought of my mother assaulting anyone is ludicrous, especially when she's been so active in trying to change soccer governance and fight for pay equity in the sport.

I lean against a wall for stability, trying to calm down amidst the crowd of students as they are leaving classes, parting around me like I'm a rock in a riverbed.

> You better start taking my calls, kid. Or I'll start making calls to other people.

A ball of hot nausea bounces through my stomach. I'm surprised to feel wetness on my cheeks when I press my knuckles against my face. For a minute, I worry it's blood from my father ripping open old wounds. But apparently, I'm just crying.

I wipe my face on my sleeve, attempting to block out the world, when I hear a soft voice call my name.

"Wyatt? Are you okay?"

I open my eyes to see Fern standing before me, her brow furrowed with concern. I try to force a smile, but it feels more like a grimace. "Yeah, I'm fine. Just needed some air."

She takes a step closer, her hand hesitantly reaching out to touch my arm. "You don't look fine. What happened?"

I shake my head, not wanting to burden her with my problems. "It's nothing. Just some family stuff."

Fern's gaze is steady, her voice gentle but firm. She

bites her plump lip, and I shudder. "Wyatt, I can see that you're upset. You can talk to me."

"Can I?" I take a deep breath, weighing the options. Something about Fern's presence, the warmth in her eyes, makes me want to trust her.

"I heard from my father," I say, my voice tight. "He's not ... he's not a good man. He said some things and made some threats. It just brought up a lot of bad memories."

Fern's hand tightens on my arm, her touch grounding me. "I'm so sorry, Wyatt. Do you want me to call anybody for you?"

I shake my head, swallowing past the lump in my throat. "I'm fine. Seriously. He's just a blowhard. I'm going to head home." She looks skeptical. "My roommates are there."

Fern's voice is still soft, so it is different from her tone in class. "I know we don't know each other that well, but I'm here for you. If you ever need to talk or just need someone to listen."

Her words wrap around me, soothing the raw edges of my pain. I manage a small smile. "Thank you, Fern. That means a lot."

She returns the smile, her hand sliding down to gently squeeze mine. "Anytime."

We stand there for a moment, the silence between us comfortable and understanding. "I really messed up a few months ago and reached out to him."

She winces. "I went through a phase like that. Expecting my dad to be a real adult. Like TV dads."

I nod. "I figured ... I hadn't talked to him in over ten years. Maybe I was misremembering all the things that happened before Mom left him. It was dumb of me to think we'd just reconnect like friends or something. All I did was remind him that Mom has money now."

Her eyes are warm and understanding. "I'm sorry, Wyatt. That must have really hurt. And now he's … being cruel?"

I nod and don't say anything else because what is there to say? Finally, I take a deep breath and straighten my shoulders. "So, yeah, I'm going home now. Thanks, teach." I add that last part as a reminder to myself that she's offering this support as part of some duty from the university. I'm pretty sure they all have to look out for students' well-being. But she looks a little stricken when I say it.

Fern nods, regardless. "Okay. My offer stands. Whenever you need it."

"I'll remember," I promise. "And Fern … thanks again. For being here."

She smiles, warm and genuine. She gives a wave and crosses the street toward a crowded bus stop. I look away and wander home, trying to forget.

CHAPTER 10
FERN

IT TAKES me ages to calm down after teaching my recitation section every Friday. I know the material pretty well, and I think I'm doing a good job of keeping the students engaged and learning the material. But it's just *so much work* to keep my cool in front of them and project a confident aura.

Especially when I've got Wyatt sitting there, hot and vulnerable. I found myself wanting to wrap him in my arms the other day, even though I knew I couldn't. I need to remember to look up resources for students like him who are having issues with their families. I'm sure the other teaching assistants are probably better equipped to handle those things. All I had to offer him was a stupid hand squeeze and listening ear.

I have so much riding on this class going well...so much. The stress of that alone would make my back sweat but add in Wyatt sitting in the circle of students each week, staring me down with his dark eyes. He always looks like he did when we were naked together—intense, dirty, vulnerable, and dominant all mixed together.

My phone buzzes in my bag, shaking me out of my thoughts. It's a text from Thora about meeting up for lunch. I smile and send her a thumbs-up. I have just enough time to sit in my cubicle across from Professor Yoon's office and chip away at my own coursework.

Saving my easier classes for my final semester was a pretty slick move. Sure, I had to work like a maniac last semester on all the advanced math classes, but I needed those completed before my grad school application anyway. I'm staring down a few months of a more relaxed pace.

I've been really enjoying my art class, which surprises me because I pretty much never thought about art once before this. This week, I've been thrilled to read about how fractals are present in the work of famous artists like Jackson Pollock and Katsushika Hokusai.

I happily spend an hour on my paper for art history before my timer goes off to meet Thora in the cafeteria. She's already sprawled out at a table with a bowl of soup when I arrive. I don't want to interrupt her since she hasn't yet heard about her law school acceptance, and I know she's a bit of a mess. By the time I wait in line for my sandwich, and make my way over to her, she's got ink on her nose and has propped one of her pre-law textbooks on her empty soup bowl.

"Hey," I whisper, sliding into the seat across from her. "You gonna make it?"

She looks up at me and blows her hair out of her eyes. "To be determined. Ugh, is it past noon already?" She glances around at the crowded cafeteria.

I nod, mouth full of sandwich. I swallow and tell her, "I don't mind a working lunch if you need to get caught up.

I'm reading about fractals as a tool to identify forgery in fine art."

Thora rolls her eyes. "I have no idea what any of that means. None of it."

I laugh. "That's okay." I wave a hand at her spread of books. "What are you frazzled about?"

"Ugh, I'm in this stupid argument class that's half full of jocks who give zero shits and half full of pre-law students who really need the credits. And, of course, the professor stuck me with another pre-law student for this project."

I frown. "Why is that bad?"

"Because now I have to actually collaborate and talk through the problems." She slams a book shut and picks up her soup bowl. I laugh as she licks at the rim. "God, this is good. So salty. Anyway, if I had a jock partner, I could just do the whole thing my way, be in charge, make sure it's all perfect. You know?"

I do know. We get along because we both have that desperate need for perfection and control. If we mess up, we both know the stakes and how even one lousy grade can set off a staircase of unintended consequences. I pat her hand. "I'm sure you and the other pre-law asshole will make a fine argument about ..." I glance at the books she's been packing in her bag. "...the effectiveness of standardized tests. Thora that sounds boring as hell."

She nods. "It is. Did I mention we couldn't come to an agreement about our topic, and the professor had to *assign* one to us?" Shaking her head, Thora fixes her ponytail and then leans forward on her elbows, chin in her hands. "How was recitation today?"

I flush. She notices. "And what was he wearing this

time? Maybe those mesh shirts they put on when they break into teams? With nothing underneath?"

"Thora Jansson, stop it right now!" The damage is done, of course. I'm thinking about Wyatt in athletic shorts and a mesh tank top, staring at me like he does in class.

She stands up and gestures for me to follow her. "You're the one who said you need to figure out how to let loose this semester. You haven't even gone to a party yet, have you?"

I shake my head, following her out of the cafeteria. "I think I already had my fun. And like I said, this art class is pretty cool."

"Jesus, Fern. One night of nooky and a class that's not impossible is not a formula for a fun final semester."

"Oh, like you're out there doing keg stands and snorting coke."

She laughs at me. "Is that how you think of fun? Drugs and being upside down?"

I shrug. "What do I know about relaxing?"

She links her arm with mine. "Come on. I don't have class 'til three. Let's go into the hotel across the street and steal desserts from the conference room."

I swat at her. "We can't do that. People paid for those."

"Yeah, and we're usually the ones being paid to serve them and clean them up. You know how many are usually leftover." Thora tugs my hand across Fifth Avenue into the fancy university building where—I don't even know what sorts of business people gather at these events. She's right that we're usually working with the catering staff. Hesitantly, I follow her into one of the ballrooms. She smiles and waves at the men and women in suits, making a beeline for the dessert buffet. Before I can blink, we're back outside, each holding a tiny plastic cup of mousse with a tiny wooden spoon.

Thora dots chocolate on my nose with her spoon. "See? Wasn't that fun? And nobody was eating them anyway."

Eventually, I relax enough to swallow the dessert. We sit side by side on a black metal bench, watching students rush past en route to class, eating decadent sweets. And I really do feel more relaxed.

Thora wanders off for her afternoon class, and I head home, wishing I'd saved some of the mousse to share with my mom. Inspired, I look up a recipe for mousse on my phone and stop at the store to grab the ingredients.

Another movie night with Mom and fancy dessert sounds like just the thing to kick off ... well, a weekend full of coursework and not entirely relaxing. I'm fidgety because I'm used to working at the bar, but when I couldn't take weeknight shifts anymore, they filled my position with another bartender. It'll be okay. Soon enough.

CHAPTER 11

WYATT

MY COUSIN WES uses the term "competency boner" when discussing his girlfriend. Cara is one of the best soccer players in the world, and Wes was a goner for her the second he saw her in action. Well, not only is Fern Montgomery a fantastic bartender … she's also a really fucking good teacher. Sitting in class listening to her explain how to solve equations like nothing has me more than half-hard.

It's been at least three weeks, and I try not to make eye contact with her, recite the quadratic equation, and think about my steps for taking penalty kicks, but it's hopeless. I'm hot for this teacher.

I stare at my lap until she says, "Okay, that's it for this week. Let me know if you have any questions about the exam."

Shit. The exam. I've been so busy fretting about what damage my father might cause that I've really been struggling when it comes to my studies. I'm not a terrible student, but math has never been my best subject. My family is always saying sports use a lot of math skills, and

I guess they're right, but I don't see how that translates to absolute value or whatever it's called.

I hustle out of the classroom, wondering what social activity my cousins are going to rope me into this weekend. I've been a lot less grumpy about driving their asses to bars since I got the vague hope that Fern might be working as a bartender, but I think she stopped doing that now that she's got this teaching gig.

I emerge from the elevator to find Odin and Stellan sprawled on the wooden benches in the lobby of the classroom tower. "Wyatt!" Odin looks up from his phone as Stellan yells my name. "We're doing a Costco run. You're driving."

I roll my eyes at them. "Why do I always have to drive? This isn't even a drinking event."

Odin shrugs. "Your car has the most cargo space. We need like 35 gallons of cereal, plus toilet paper."

I sink onto the bench next to him. "We are four guys living in an apartment. How much toilet paper do we possibly need?"

Stellen starts counting on his fingers. "It's been months since we restocked, man."

"Yeah, and I'll be graduating in a few months. The last thing I want to do is pack toilet paper when I go to Mexico."

Odin shakes his head and stands, offering me a hand to tug me to my feet. "You act like my brothers aren't lined up to take over the lease when you graduate this spring, dude. There will be Stags in that spot for years."

I walk beside them in the cold for the few blocks back to our apartment, where we dump our backpacks and fight over who will drive to the store. A series of texts comes through from my mom, asking if I'll have dinner with her tonight instead of Sunday. I show the phone to my roommates. "I will drive, but only because you fuckers are going to unload on the curb, and I'll go on from there to hang out with my mom."

Odin rubs his palms together. "That means you guys won't be at family dinner on Sunday, which means more of Aunt Alice's chicken for me."

I punch his shoulder. "I might show up Sunday, too. Just because my parents are out scouting or whatever doesn't mean I can't come."

———

An hour later, my car has been stuffed to the ceiling with packaged snacks and then unloaded in a snow squall; I'm finally on my way to the soccer stadium to grab my mom. I wave at the parking attendant, who has known me since Mom got this job when I was four years old, and I pull into a spot right by the stadium offices.

I could text Mom that I'm outside, but I enjoy going into her office. As a kid, I used to run up and down these halls, sneaking into the locker room where my dad and the other guys on the team would let me score on them. Now, Dad's retired from playing and is coaching the men's team, and the city has added a women's pro team to share the facility.

I start sweating when another message comes in from Nick—another number I haven't blocked yet.

> You know it's slander for you to talk about me in the papers. I see these articles coming up. Big shot kid looking for a big contract, and the reporters gotta mention some bullshit from 20 years ago? Fuck you. I'm going to sue you.

A lump forms in my throat. I don't know what slander means, really, but asking my lawyer-uncle about it would lead to more questions than I know how to answer.

How the hell could I be on the hook for some reporter looking up public information that half the world already knows? I haven't let that man's name cross my lips to a reporter. Ever. I need to figure some shit out before I can deal with any of this, so I block the number and go looking for my mom.

She steps through the door of her office just as I'm shaking away this current wave of dread. "Wyatt! Come here, you look freezing." Mom wraps her arms around me and looks surprised that I'm taller than her, as if I haven't been taller than her for ten years now. "Well, I thought I could warm you up, but I guess we'll just blast the heat in your car. Where do you want to eat?"

I shrug, and Mom suggests we try the robot sushi place, where all the food goes by on a conveyor belt. "Yeah, that sounds fun."

I drive, and Mom talks about her roster leading up to the Olympics. She always played midfield, like my dad and me, and I like hearing her assess the women's national team. We get to the restaurant, and Mom keeps talking.

I think this is going to be a pretty easy meal with her until Mom grabs two plates of California rolls and holds them out of my reach. "I talked to Brian." I groan and she slides me one of the plates. "Why are you postponing a contract offer? And he said you turned down an endorse-ment opportunity?"

I take a bite of the sushi, but it all tastes like sand in my mouth. I can't tell her I'm waiting to sign a contract until I figure out if Nick can really sue me. Suppose signing something so publicly will set him off bringing up lies about her and Dad. "I've got some complications at the moment. But I'm handling it."

"That's what Brian said you said. I just don't know why you'd sit on something like that, honey. It's not like our family lacks lawyers who can help. Whatever it is. Uncle Tim is a huge donor to your school. I'm sure what-ever is going on, he could—"

I snap at my mom. "I said I'm handling it." Her head jerks back, her expression pained. I sigh. "I also need to figure out what I want and what my career is going to look like. I want to begin my professional career as I plan to continue. Brian is always talking about building a brand. Maybe I'm not a cereal flake ambassador. Maybe I'm more of a deodorant icon."

Mom grins and shakes her head. My Dad and his brother Ty did a spot for Old Spice a few years ago, talking about Stag Swagger. "As long as you have a plan, Wyatt. But please know Dad and I are here for you. You can tell us anything." A silence hangs between us, and I wonder if she's thinking what I'm thinking—that I spent a ton of time in therapy telling first the psychologist and then Mom and Dad all the things that happened to me when Nick had visitation.

I've always walked around feeling like a stain on this family. The Stag family is full of massive success—profes-sional athletes, incredible artists, and writers ... I know they don't mean to make me feel like the dark-haired stepchild, but that's precisely what I am.

———

I drive Mom home after dinner, endure extra-long hugs from her in the driveway, and head to my place to get caught up on my schoolwork while the apartment is empty. Except it's no use. I can't concentrate on my history paper, and no matter what I try, I can't figure out how to solve the practice problems Fern gave us to prepare for the exam on Monday.

I slam my notebook closed, and a piece of paper flutters out—the syllabus. I look at it as I go to shove it back in the folder and see an online forum for the recitation class. Chances are pretty slim that Fern or anyone would be on there at eight on a Friday night, but I log in mainly to satisfy my curiosity.

Sure enough, I'm the only student in the room; everyone else's name is grayed out ... except a bright green dot next to Instructor.

Fern.

Hey. I type in the chat window quickly, realizing I should elaborate. *I'm stuck on the problem about filling the bags of sugar.*

I stare at the screen for a few breaths. I'm about to slam my laptop shut and watch reality television instead when I see some floating dots appear in the chat window. Oh shit, Fern is typing back. I try not to imagine her in comfortable clothes at home, maybe not wearing a bra, perhaps those fantastic tits shaking a bit as she types furiously to help me.

Where are you stuck?

My lips part, thinking about her naked even as she's trying to help me with math. Why is this hot for me? I'm seriously fucked in the head. She's trying to help me with my math homework; it is her job. Fern seems perfectly capable of forgetting our night together, treating me just like any other student. Which is what I am. A student who is stuck on a math problem about weighing bags of sugar: *I got the heaviest possible bag, but I don't know how the equation can find the lightest possible bag of sugar.*

Fern asks me a few questions, which initially frustrates me because wouldn't it be easier if she just told me what I'm missing… but finally, I see what to do on my own. I actually feel the tension leave my shoulders as I type a formula into the chat box, and then when Fern types, *perfect! You got it!* I feel like I just scored a fucking goal in the last instant of a game.

Thanks so much, Fern.

I bite my lip. *I mean Ms. Montgomery. Thank you for helping me on a Friday night.*

My pleasure. Does she really mean that? Oh, god, I can't think about pleasuring Fern.

I stare at the screen, unsure if I'm expected to respond if she's still sitting there. My heart thunders in my chest, but I type, *You're really good at explaining this stuff. I mean it.*

Thanks, Wyatt. I appreciate that. Good luck on Monday's exam. Have a good weekend.

Again, I should close the computer. I should walk away. But her instructor dot stays green. She's still sitting there on her end. It's not like I can type anything I'm really thinking, especially not on an official university server. But damn, do I want to know what she's wearing, what she's doing after this, why she'd be monitoring the online support forum on a Friday.

By the time her green dot turns gray, I'm fully hard, aching in my jeans, remembering how she looked spread open on my bed, how she tasted when she was so nervous about being sweaty. I close my computer and move to my bed, wishing I could still smell and feel her there as I unzip my jeans, take myself in my hand, and relieve myself to the memory of Fern Montgomery's O-face.

CHAPTER 12

FERN

MOM COMES up behind me at the table, leaning over my shoulder to kiss the top of my head and peek at my computer monitor. "You're doing work on a Friday night?"

I shrug. "I'm usually *working working* on Friday nights."

Mom pulls up the other chair at our small table for two. "I'm glad you have a bit more room in your schedule this semester. I thought you'd go do fun teenager stuff, though."

I try not to roll my eyes. "Mom, I'm 22 years old."

She winces. "Okay, okay. But still. Where's Thora?"

I suck on my teeth. "I think she's working the hockey game tonight. She got one of the bar stands that has a tip cup, so she was excited for that." Neither Mom nor I need to mention that I don't have other friends. Everyone from high school is either involved in their adult lives by now, with kids or full-time jobs, or else far away at their colleges, working weekend gigs to supplement their scholarships.

Mom tilts her chin toward the computer. "Well, what are you working on? I saw you smiling at the computer when I came for a drink of water."

I flush. "I was working on a paper, but then one of my math students was in the forum asking for help."

Mom tilts her head, looking at me strangely. "One of your students, hmm? What's that about?"

I wave a hand and close the computer. "He's someone I knew from before … one of the regulars at Fuel Up. It's been … weird having him in the class."

Mom frowns. "Fern, I don't need to tell you what can happen if you lose yourself to a man."

I press my fingers into the scratched surface of the table. We've had it as long as I can remember, and I'm pretty sure it came to us nicked and scuffed. "You don't need to tell me again, no. And like you said, Mom, I live like a monk. So, there's nothing to worry about."

Mom crosses her arms. "It's not that I don't want you to go out and experience dating and love and adventure." She sighs. "It's just all so … fragile. You know? Like there's only a tiny icicle between having a good time and making a choice you can't unmake."

I nod. We've had this conversation a lot. Too many times. This conversation is why I work so hard at my studies, but it's also why I went wild on New Year's Eve, and now I'm having to pretend like I'm not a hot mess every time I see or even think about Wyatt Moyer.

I sigh. "I'm going to go to bed. I love you."

I reach for her hand, and she squeezes mine. "Love you, too."

———

In the morning, I feel restless in our apartment. Mom is at work, and Thora is most likely still asleep. I take the train downtown and grab a bus to campus, head into my usual spot in the library, and freeze in my tracks when I see the very cause of my unsettled state.

Wyatt sprawls in a chair by the wall of windows overlooking Forbes Avenue. His long legs, clad as usual in gray sweats, seem to take up the entire floor. He wears a university t-shirt despite the January chill, and his baseball hat is tugged low over his eyes. His dark hair peeks out a bit from the edges of the hat. I wonder if he's due for a cut or just likes it shaggy that way. And I can't be wondering such things about one of my students.

I pause and look around, trying to find another place to sit and get some work done, but something causes Wyatt to look up, and his eyes catch mine. I have one of those moments where the rest of the room fades away, it's like I'm peering down a tube. All I can see is Wyatt, framed by bright daylight, smiling at me.

"Fern! Hey."

I nod and look over my shoulder again. Now that he's seen me, is it rude if I don't sit near him? Instructors sit in libraries with their students. I've done it myself lots of times. I sigh and walk toward the seat next to him, opposite a low table with just enough space for both our notebooks. "Hi yourself. I don't usually see you here …"

He shakes his head. "Well, technically, I'm supposed to be at cardio this morning, but I have a meeting with my agent later, and … you probably don't care about any of that. Sorry. Hi."

I swallow and tuck my hair back behind my ears even though none of it had come loose from my ponytail. I wish I had tried a little harder with my appearance today, but

I'm in old jeans, an old bar t-shirt, and a huge sweater that probably has holes. "I don't mind. Will you get in trouble for missing cardio? With the team?"

Wyatt sets his book down on the table. I see that it's the same one he was reading a few weeks ago, when I met him. But now he's nearly done with it. "I won't get in trouble, no. I would have entered the MLS draft and been gone from here, but I have some shit I need to finish up." He shakes his head. "That's not what you want to hear about, either."

I fuss around with my bag, pulling out my pencil sharpener and scrap paper I rescued from the recycling bin in my classroom. "You mentioned a hard time changing your name. What's the problem with that?"

"You really want to know?" Wyatt leans forward toward me like he really wants to tell me about this, like he needs someone to listen.

"Sure. I'm a pretty good problem solver."

He laughs. "Yeah, that's true. Well. Like I said, my bio dad is a piece of shit. My step-dad has always wanted to adopt me, but dirtbag wouldn't relinquish his parental rights. It was a whole fucking thing my parents dealt with for years." His face shifts, like the memories make him uncomfortable. "I couldn't get a passport. You need both parents to sign for that to leave the country. So, my whole family couldn't travel unless they left me at home. Which, to their credit, they never once complained about where I could hear them." He puffs out a breath. "But my parents are both heavily involved with the national soccer teams, and Dad competed in the Olympics a few times…Mom coaches all over Europe. They always had to leave me and my sister home with family."

"You have a sister?" I'm not sure why this is what I

latch onto in that whole heartbreaking story, but the rest of it is so foreign to me. A family that competes internationally in sports? Forget about it. My dad can't even hold down a job.

Wyatt nods. "Birdie. Yeah. She's an elite soccer player, too. Anyway, the second I turned 18 we got the passport sorted out. But I wanted to change my name, to be like the rest of my family." He bites his lip, scooting his chair closer, like someone might be listening to him. "I went to try and do it myself, and they make you run an ad in the newspaper that you're changing your name and offer a number if someone objects."

"What? That's nuts." I never heard of anything like that. "My mom didn't have to do that when she married my dad…not that that lasted longer than a few seconds."

Wyatt waves a hand. "If you're married or divorced, it's easy. But otherwise, they think you're trying to avoid credit card debt, so you have to go through hoops. I didn't hoop properly, and I wound up poking the bear."

I frown. "Your bio-father, you mean?"

He nods. "Yeah." He groans. "It's so dumb. I called him thinking–I don't know. That we'd be buddies or something? I wanted to tip him off that I was changing my name."

I shrug. "That doesn't sound dumb. I always hoped my dad would be my buddy, but I gave up trusting that he'd ever show up when he said he was going to."

Wyatt drags a hand through his hair. "Yeah, well, once Nick caught wind of what was happening, he started threatening me."

A chill runs through me, and I hug my arms to my chest. There's something about the look in Wyatt's eye:

this big, muscular athlete with a wealthy family and resources being scared of someone. "What did he say?"

Wyatt shakes his head. "I'm not getting into all that. I just can't have him stirring up shit for my parents. That's what he'd do, mostly. Create bad press. Tell lies. Drag my mom's name through the mud again." He sighs like the weight of the entire library is crashing down on his strong shoulders. "She worked too hard to get away from him and make something of herself, to get me away from him."

I bite my lip and tap my finger on my lap. "But you're kind of a big deal athlete, from what I hear."

He grins at this. "You've been hearing stuff about me, Fern?"

I roll my eyes. "Knock it off. That's my point. People talk about you."

He nods. "Yeah, and every time they do, it's only a matter of time before they run a search, and news articles come up about poor Wyatt, the kid who had to be rescued by the police." Wyatt looks over my shoulder and out the window at the bustling city. Students pour out of the 7/11 and the Dunkin' Donuts. Tourists stop at a sidewalk cart to buy university t-shirts. Here, we're just two people under a lot of pressure, in different ways, trying to keep our noses down and get through it all.

A fist of anguish punches my heart, thinking of a little boy going through that again and again his whole life as that scary incident comes up in every news article about him playing soccer. "That sounds awful. The police thing."

He nods. "I was thinking maybe I blew it out of proportion in my mind, you know? But once I actually reached out to him … he showed me that I had it right all along."

I should hug this man. Student or not ... he's hurting. Unsure what to do, I reach out and squeeze his knee. "You couldn't have known that he'd threaten your family. It's been years. I get why you thought he'd work on himself."

Wyatt puffs out a laugh. I grin. "I have fantasies about my dad going on meds or something. Getting a therapist. Getting a job... buying me a birthday card." I shake my head. "What will you do after you graduate? You said you have an agent?"

Wyatt swallows, and when he meets my eyes, he looks more vulnerable than I felt the night he took me home. "I'm trying to play internationally. But I need to sort out my name to sign my contract as Wyatt Moyer. It's important to me."

We stare at one another for a long time. "Can't your agent help with that?"

Wyatt groans and sinks lower into his chair, dragging a palm down his face. "He's my dad's agent, too. And my cousin's. Like I said, I can't have any of this impacting my family. It's something I really want to do on my own. Like ... a lot of stuff has been handed to me over the years. It feels like the least I can do is sort out my legal problems."

I'm not sure what to say in response to that. I know family law is a horrifying ordeal. My dad hasn't even been unpleasant or vindictive, and it was still a nightmare for my mom for a long time. So much was out of her control, always. And she always felt like she was being scrutinized by the court. I can't imagine how much more stressful that would have been if my father had been abusive.

Neglectful, sure, but never abusive. I want to reach out to Wyatt, to gather him in my arms and tell him I understand. But that feels like crossing a line, so I just press my lips together and nod. "Thank you," I stammer. "For telling me all that. I won't betray your trust."

He nods, takes a deep breath, and stares up at the ceiling while he blows it out. Then he points at his notebook. "Feel like talking me through *those* problems again? I'm not feeling good about the exam."

A warm current flows through me at the thought of helping Wyatt, of working closely with him on the language of the universe. "Sure. Tell me where you're the most stuck."

———

We spend the next few hours talking through the various word problems and I figure out that Wyatt's been forgetting how to count negative numbers. I draw a few number line sketches on his scratch paper, and it's like flipping a switch for him. He solves the rest of the problems quickly and finally jumps to his feet, pumping his fist. "Hell yeah!" He holds his hand out, I think, for a high five, and I slap his palm tentatively. And then my stomach gurgles louder than his celebration whoop. "Oh, crap. What time is it?" Wyatt looks at his expensive smartwatch. "Want to go grab lunch? The least I can do is buy you a sandwich for helping me on a weekend."

I wave a hand. "I packed. And you don't need to thank me. It's my job to help."

Wyatt puts a hand on his hip, scowling down at me. "It is definitely not your job to help on a Friday night or a Saturday. Come on." He beckons with his hand and reaches for my bag. "We can have a very public sandwich. You can tell me about your ..." He glances down at the notebook I never even cracked open. "… trigonometric identities. What does that mean, anyway?"

I open my mouth to explain, and he holds up a finger. "Tell me at lunch. Come on, Fern. Please?"

Then he flashes puppy eyes at me, and I throw all my reservations on the ground and stomp on them in my sensible, well-worn sneakers as I stand up to accept lunch with my student.

CHAPTER 13
WYATT

FERN SEEMS JUST as uncomfortable being seen or recognized as I am, so I suggest a diner a few blocks from the main drag. I tip my chin at the host, who is bussing tables, and Fern and I settle into one of the tall booths near the back.

Just as I watch Fern shrug out of her coat, a flustered server drops off a pair of laminated menus, still damp from a wipe-down, and plunks red plastic water cups in front of us. "Be back in a few," they say, hurrying off to another table. Fine with me.

I don't need to study the menu. I always get a grilled chicken breast with broccoli and a side of wild rice if I'm in the off-season, which I am right now. I pretend to study the menu, but really, I'm staring at Fern. She's so damn pretty, in addition to being insanely capable. Her dark hair and eyes stand out against her fair skin—Fern's complexion is almost like porcelain, but I know there's nothing fragile about her.

And god, she's curvy and soft. But never delicate. She has a wide smile she doesn't use very often. I sigh. She's been pretty clear about the stakes if she gets in trouble with her teaching gig. I shouldn't be trying to get her to smile at me.

The server comes back while Fern is frowning at the menu. I kick her gently under the table. "Remember, this is my treat to thank you for the help with the absolute value stuff."

She rolls her eyes, and the server looks back and forth between us. "You guys ready to order?" They tap a pen on an old-school restaurant notebook. That's why I like this place. No digital anything. I don't even think they take credit cards. It's dimly lit, always full, and the food is pretty good.

I glance at the server and give them my order, trying to adjust my pants in response to Fern licking her lip as she settles on what to eat. "I think I want the Reuben," she says like she's not sure. Man, how long has it been since I ate one of those? I make a mental note to treat myself in celebration once I secure a contract.

The server takes our menus, and they rush off to hand the slip to the kitchen staff. Fern folds her hands on the table and looks at me with those huge eyes of hers. "So, you're eating healthy stuff, but you're not in season, but you're skipping workouts and trying to get a professional contract? Is that about it?"

I laugh. "I know it all sounds insane. It's just what I'm used to. It's actually been pretty easy to eat clean in my family since all four of us are in elite athletics. And my Aunt Alice is a chef, so she spoils us all."

"Oh man, a chef in the family would be my undoing." Fern reaches for her water, and I can't help but stare at those full lips wrapped around the paper straw. She frowns and pulls it from her glass. "I can't handle how these feel in my mouth once they get wet." She picks up the cup and takes a sip, and it's much less evocative, which I guess is good for my still-tight pants.

"What about you," I ask her. "You said something about a fellowship?"

Fern nods. "I applied for a bunch of them. It's not like I can go to grad school without full funding. But I really want to study in London."

I lean forward, fascinated. "Why London?"

She beams and absolutely glows in the low light of this deli. "Imperial College in London is one of the best places in the world to study algebraic geometry."

I snort. "I don't even know what that is!"

Fern waves a hand. "Advanced math stuff. But the connections would be incredible. Cutting-edge research in cryptography and cybersecurity. Financial engineering. Gah!" She shimmies her shoulders, looking adorably excited. "A whole world of opportunities."

I nod. "And you didn't have a ton of opportunities before."

"Yeah." She shrugs. "You know how it can be. It sounds like you started out with a single mom..." I nod. Fern continues, saying, "Mom always wanted to study finance. She's incredible with numbers. She and my dad met in high school, got pregnant, got married, and tried to make it work with community college. Still, they didn't have a ton of support, and..." Fern drifts off and looks up at a restaurant employee who slides our plates on the table and practically takes off at a run to gather more from the counter at the kitchen window.

I slide her plate closer to her and grab my own, adding, "And your dad couldn't handle when shit got hard, so your mom made do."

Fern nods. I lift my water glass and hold it out toward her. "To strong women." I wink as she clinks her cup against mine. We have a lot in common, even though it doesn't seem like it from the outside. Sure, I had a lot going my way for the majority of my life. But the baggage of the early years is still weighing me down in a big way that I can see Fern understands. She doesn't seem grouchy and moody about her struggles, though. She just digs in and works around the clock toward her goal.

Fern picks up her sandwich, the gooey sauerkraut and sauce dripping out on the side of her hand, and takes a bite. And she releases a sound I heard a few weeks ago when I had my head between her thighs. "Shit, Fern, it's no wonder I like spending time with you."

Fern chews, blushing, and frantically reaches for napkins. "This is a mess," she whispers, and I think she means more than the sandwich. I'm about to say something else I shouldn't, something flirty and inappropriate, but a pair of students walks down the aisle toward the bathroom, and they recognize me.

"Hey! You're Wyatt from the Viper soccer team, right?" I close my eyes, take a deep breath, and nod. "Man, you had a phenomenal season! Hey, can I get an autograph?" The one guy reaches forward and snatches Fern's spare napkin, sliding it my way.

She stares at him and his companion, wide-eyed, unused to having her meals interrupted by fans. They look over at her and quickly glance back at me. I don't like that they don't say hello to her. Sure, she's not famous, but she's clearly someone important to me if I'm sitting here with her at a restaurant. Instead, the shorter of the two guys looks at Fern and asks, "You got a pen we can borrow?"

Fern's mouth works up and down, and I can tell she's about to reach for her bag to dig for a pen, but I hold up a hand. "Hey, guys, we can do a quick selfie, but please don't inconvenience my friend or take her things." I slide the napkin back toward Fern as the taller guy nods and hands me his phone.

I extend an arm to get the three of us in the photo. No way am I asking Fern to take it. I smile, tight-lipped, and hand the guy his phone back, barely acknowledging them as they walk off.

"Wow," Fern says, chewing on another bite of sandwich. I scowl. "You really don't like getting approached by fans, do you?"

"Was it obvious?"

She laughs.

I shake my head and spear a bite of chicken. I chew, swallow, and reach for my water. As I do, my hand brushes Fern's as she reaches for her water at the same time. I stare down at the place where our skin touches, feeling searing jolts of electricity run through me. It's like a pinched nerve but in a really good way.

In a moment of impulse, I lose all sense of … well, sense, and I lean forward, reaching for Fern, like I'm going to pull her face close to me and kiss her right here in the restaurant. For the briefest moment, I think she's going to reciprocate, but she pulls back and starts shaking her head. She stiffens.

"Wyatt," she whispers. "We can't do that. You can't do that. I'm your TA, and we need to have boundaries."

I nod. "I'm sorry," I tell her, and I'm about to say a whole lot more when my phone rings. It's the loud, brassy ring I assigned to Brian, my agent. I sigh. "I'm sorry," I repeat, gesturing at the phone in my hand.

She nods and takes another bite of the her sandwich. I stare at her eating as I accept the call. Brian doesn't even wait to be greeted; he just launches into news of a potential contract offer from a team in Mexico. I know Fern can hear him. I know everyone in the deli can hear him.

Fern takes one more bite of the sandwich and shrugs her arms back into her coat. I hold a hand over the phone. "You don't have to go," I say quietly.

She shakes her head and places a palm on my shoulder. I feel the warmth again, the sizzle, but I know her intention is not to encourage that type of energy. "You should talk to your agent. Thank you so much for the food, Wyatt. I'll see you in class."

She makes her way out of the crowded restaurant as Brian rattles on and on about the money we're going to earn together, about the suntan I'll get in Guadalajara. I can't manage to rustle up excitement for this opportunity, especially knowing I'm no closer than I was before to sorting out my legal name. I barely pay attention as Brian talks through his plan to woo the team. Despite the heavy odor of fried food and grilled meat, I still imagine I can smell Fern and her snow-dusted hair.

My mind reels from the disappointment of not kissing her, from the opportunity I might have to let slip away, from all of it. Eventually, I toss a bunch of money on the table and walk out, making my way home where at least my cousins can distract me with their carefree nonsense.

CHAPTER 14
FERN

MY HEART RACES as I rush from the restaurant in search of Thora. I make a beeline for Fuel Up and sure enough, she's behind the bar washing glasses, getting ready for happy hour. She glances up when the bell rings above the door as I enter, and I must look frightened because she dashes over to me and wraps me in a hug.

"What the hell happened?" She brushes my hair back from my face and studies me like she's looking for bruises. I don't need to tell her they're all internal.

I take a deep breath and blurt, "I went to lunch with Wyatt, and he tried to kiss me, and I panicked."

She laughs and shakes her head, clutching at her chest. "Fern. I thought something actually bad happened to you. Jesus." Thora walks back to the bar, slapping a towel over one shoulder and continuing to shake her head.

I follow and slide my butt into a stool, my mind racing. The thought of Wyatt's lips on mine sends surges of heat through my veins, but the fear of the consequences of kissing a student is like a bucket of cold water, shocking me back to reality. "I'm serious, Thora. This could be really bad."

She squints at me, considering. "But you like him?"

I groan. "I really do. He makes me feel …" I try to verbalize the connection I feel to him, but I just shrug. "He's just great."

Thora winks. "Doesn't hurt that he's fly as hell and probably has an ass you could bounce darts off of."

I press my palms to the bar and purse my lips. "I can't stop thinking about him. Not just the physical stuff. All of it."

Thora sighs. "I get it. He's hot, and you two have chemistry, and it sounds like he's a sexy, moody orgasm vending machine."

I wince. "That's all true and accurate. But …"

Thora's eyes soften. "I know it's not just about the physical stuff, Fern, and that you're focused on what's at stake here. Your career, your dreams. But you also deserve to have fun and feel good."

I sniff. "I hoped you'd tell me to be careful and that I've worked too hard to risk it all for a guy."

Thora grabs a clean glass and starts polishing it with the towel, winking. "Not my style." The familiar clink of glasses and hum of conversation fill the air as more patrons trickle in. The bell above the door tinkles again and a group of students makes their way toward the televisions along the back wall, showing pro hockey and basketball games. Thora raises her brows. "That's my cue to get pouring. You going to be okay?"

I flap a hand at her. "Yeah. I just needed to vent about it."

"What kind of bartender would I be if I wasn't here for

you when you needed to vent?" Thora grins and sets a pitcher under the tap.

I say goodbye and leave the bar to bury myself in class-work. As I head home, I try desperately not to think about my moodiest student. I take a deep breath, pushing thoughts of Wyatt from my mind and shaking away the echoes of his intense gaze and the warmth of his touch.

———

Monday morning arrives, gray and frigid, matching my mood as I make my way to campus and the algebra lecture hall. "Is Dr. Yoon here yet?" A student is waiting outside the lecture hall when I arrive early to set things up for the exam. Their eyes dart from their watch to me and back, cheeks flushed.

My arms are full of test papers, so I try to communicate with my eyes that I need help opening the door. They do not get the hint. I sigh. "No, they will be arriving in a bit. Could you grab the door for me?"

"Oh. Sorry." The student opens the door and follows me down the aisle toward the lectern, asking what will be on the test and whether they can look over the paper before we begin.

I set the stack on the podium, letting my forearm cover the papers. "I'm really sorry, but it's a timed test. I can't let you look before the exam begins."

Their demeanor shifts—jaw set, body stiff. I can tell they're frustrated. I see a spark in their eye, and my heart rate increases. Are they going to hulk out over this? I try to think of how I'd respond at work to a customer who gives me the willies. Tending bar, I usually have a bouncer I make eye contact with, and I don't have to explain a damn thing.

Here, I'm apparently on my own with a kid who seems on the verge of a mental health crisis. They're about to begin a tirade of injustice when I see a dark figure looming behind them. Wyatt is early, striding down the aisle like he can sense my discomfort from the back of the room.

"Can I borrow a pencil?" He asks me this, even though I can see at least three mechanical pencils sticking out of his shirt pocket.

I swallow, relieved, as the frustrated student huffs their way to a seat in the front row. I nod and reach into my bag for a pencil. Wyatt's fingers linger on mine as I hand over the yellow wood. I make eye contact—a huge mistake— and a flush creeps up my neck. I remember the charged moment at lunch, the near kiss, and I think about how artfully he handled the situation just now…appearing to rudely interrupt while actually rescuing me from a frustrated, panicked undergrad.

I like the idea of having someone swoop in, someone looking out for me, even with little stuff like this. But this is a very dangerous thing to yearn for, and I have two decades of experience with the realities of trying to count on someone else and eventually giving up on him. My mom and I are solid, but I still see the impact of how my dad messed her up—messed us both up.

Dr. Yoon enters the auditorium to a flutter of the student's questions, and Wyatt releases my hand. With a nod, he shuffles to the back of the room and sinks low in his chair, tugging that hat low over his eyes. I can't tell if he's nervous about the test. He shouldn't be. By the time we left the library, he had a great grasp of the material.

I try to listen as Dr. Yoon firmly sends the anxious

student to their seat. I need to learn to set boundaries like this if I'm going to enter academia someday. At the very least, I'll be navigating students like this in graduate school. But I can't concentrate, and Dr. Yoon actually snaps their fingers to get my attention when it's time to distribute the papers.

My hands tremble slightly as I pass out the tests, especially when I get to Wyatt's row and see his dark eyes following on my every move. I take a deep breath and remind myself to stay focused as I hand out the last of the papers.

Dr. Yoon taps on the microphone at the front of the large room. "You may begin." There's a brief roar of papers being flipped over, a flurry of pencil scratches, and then all I have to do is pace the aisles, making sure nobody is visibly cheating.

I try to keep a watchful eye on the students, but I find myself glancing at Wyatt more than I ought to. I notice things like how sexy he looks with his brow furrowed in concentration. How he taps his pencil when he's thinking. How he flexes his fingers along his thigh with the hand not holding the pencil.

The hour crawls by in a tumult of my racing heart. I'm sweating when Dr. Yoon finally announces there are five minutes left. I take my place beside the podium, and the students who have finished early file up to submit their tests. "Make sure you put your name on the front page," I say repeatedly, and a number of students retract their paper to label it after the fact.

The class period ends, and the final students make their way up front. Wyatt lingers behind, approaching me with his paper. "Thanks for all your help," he says, his voice a low rumble that vibrates every tendon in my body. I nod and look down to see he's holding out my pencil. When I close my hand around the tip to take it back, he squeezes the eraser end and grins.

A warmth spreads through my chest before I can stop it, before I can remind myself that I'm trying to leave the damn country, and the last thing I need is to feel any sort of anything for a guy, especially one who is off limits.

Wyatt leaves the lecture hall, and I get to work stacking the test papers. I turn to hand them to Dr. Yoon, who is packing up their messenger bag. "Here you go."

They glance at me. "I usually have the TA's grade the exams and only come to me with questions."

"Oh." I bite my lip. "I'm not sure I know how to distribute these to the group?"

Dr. Yoon frowns, pausing as they pack up their things to leave, and I realize just how little preparation I've had for this TA gig. Dr. Yoon shifts their weight from foot to foot, clearly in a hurry to leave, and seems frustrated to have to explain the basics to me. "Aren't you all on a group chat? An email thread?"

A lump forms in my throat. I hate feeling unprepared. "I'm not on one of those, no. How can I get the list of names of the others?"

They sigh. "I'm sorry. I have a committee presentation. I'm sure you'll figure something out, Fern. You're very bright."

They rush from the room, leaving me with the stack of tests. I close my eyes and take three deep breaths. I will go to the math department office and ask one of the admins for advice. Admins always know everything. This will be fine. They're right—I'm resourceful.

Wyatt is slumped on a bench, staring at his phone, when I open the door. I huff out a laugh. Of course, he's here. I sink onto the bench next to him, and he smiles at his phone as he continues typing. "Can't get enough of me, Montgomery?"

"Yep. That's me. Obsessed." I shuffle my bag around so I can put the stack of papers inside. "How do you feel after the test?"

"You should grade mine right now and tell me how I did." He slides his phone into the pocket with his pencils, looking at me expectantly.

"Ha. How about no. I am absolutely not getting involved in grading yours." I feel a flutter of anticipation, wondering if he'll touch me. Wanting him to touch me. Knowing he shouldn't.

As if he can sense my distress, he eases away from me on the bench. "Sorry. I'm being pushy. I just really think you're awesome."

His cheeks get small spots of pink, causing me to flush as well. I laugh. "We're both worked up over this test, I think."

He smiles. "I'll let you get to grading. See you Friday?"

I nod and watch him walk away. I gather my things and head toward the math department office, where the admin pulls a list of the other student teaching assistants for Dr. Yoon's class. When I lean on the wall outside the office to email the group about divvying up the tests, I see an unread message from Imperial College in London.

I gasp as I click to read it.

Dear Ms. Montgomery: I am delighted to inform you that you've been selected...

I stop reading and close my eyes. My heart races. Is this really happening? I hum a little bit and open my eyes, returning to the message.

...for our graduate fellowship in algebraic geometry,

including tuition remission, a monthly stipend, accommodation in our private graduate student housing, as well as a meal plan for our residential dining halls. Assuming completion of your degree and receipt of final transcripts…

I stop reading again, eyes watering. This is it. This is what I've been working for. My dreams are so close I can feel them with my fingertips. I stamp out thoughts of Wyatt and his exam and his soccer career. I need to focus on finishing this semester.

I pull up a group chat with Thora and my mom, typing three words in all caps:

I GOT IT!

Their responses come almost immediately, and I smile, knowing I'll be celebrating with them.

CHAPTER 15
FERN

THORA AND MOM flank me as we walk up Forbes Avenue in the fading daylight. I was excited that the timing worked so they could both be in the neighborhood to celebrate with me as soon as I got the note from Imperial College. Thora points at the bougie new chain restaurant with a bright sign. "This calls for milkshakes," she says, tugging us inside.

I try not to look at the price tag for three shakes—they don't even have alcohol stirred in, so why on *earth* do they cost this much—and we find a high table to sit. Mom's eyes water as she holds up her plastic cup brimming with whipped cream and cherries. "To my hardworking girl, who never takes her eye off the prize."

"Cheers to that!" Thora plucks a cookie from the top of her treat and bites into it.

I click my cup against each of theirs and savor the sweet drink. "It all feels surreal," I say after swallowing. "Like ... this has been the goal for so long. What's the goal now?"

Thora rolls her eyes. "Getting the damn degree, Montgomery. That's the goal. Do you have your student visa yet?"

I shake my head. "No, I needed the acceptance letter first."

"Oh, right." She taps her fingers on the table. "Not gonna lie, I'm anxious about my own acceptance letter now."

Mom squeezes both our forearms. "I just know you'll both be heading off to London together. Thora, what makes you want to do a law degree over there, though?"

Thora's eyes widen, and she waggles her brows. "International business, baby. I want to go everywhere. I want clients in Tokyo. I want to facilitate deals in Delhi. London is a starting place."

I set down my milkshake and squeeze Mom's hand. "Don't worry. I plan to come back stateside after my degree. I'm just looking for a very specific program expertise."

Thora laughs. "Only about 30 people in the world understand what you do with your math, babe. And that's fine because you're a beautiful algebra wizard."

Mom's eyes watery as she sips her shake. "Fern, you've always seen numbers differently from other people. I don't know where that comes from, but it's very special, and I know you've worked so hard." She dabs at her eye with a napkin.

I draw in a shuddering breath. "Mom, you've been supportive. Always. We did this together. I wish you could come with me!"

She waves a hand. "Maybe someday. For a visit." We share a grin until I feel my phone buzz in my pocket. Frowning, wondering who it could be, I glance down. It's Wyatt. I forgot I had given him my number at lunch. I press my lips together and send the call to voicemail as Thora and Mom talk about how nice it would be if Mom flew first class to see us both in London. Thora snorts. "It's not like anyone from my family will be coming over."

I slurp the last of my shake. There's no way I'll be hungry for dinner after this. "Never say never, Thor."

She squints and points at the ceiling. "The only way my parents are coming to London is if they're on the run from the law." Thora's purse begins to beep. "Ah, shit. I gotta get to the arena. I'm working the hockey game tonight."

Mom glances at her watch. "I should ride with you. I don't like to take the train too late." She looks up at me. "How long are you staying on campus, sweetheart? You said you have TA work to do this evening?"

I nod. "I want to get a head start on grading these exams alongside the other folks, get a sense of the routine and all that."

Mom frowns. "But you won't stay too late? Or splurge for a car if you do?"

There's no way I'm splurging on a ride share after we just had expensive milkshakes, but I nod my head to appease her. Public transportation is perfectly safe if you know how to use your elbows, which I do.

Mom and Thora wave and head to catch a bus toward downtown. They sandwich me in a hug on their way out of the shop, and once they're gone, I fiddle with my cup, deciding it can't hurt to listen to Wyatt's voicemail. His voice comes through the phone in a broken, muffled torrent about threats from his father and demands for money.

It's hard to ignore the undercurrent of panic in Wyatt's

voice as I listen to his message, and I head instinctively toward his apartment a few blocks away, worried.

———

I knock on the door, hoping it's the correct one, and am greeted by a giant who shouts something about food delivery. "Sorry," I mutter. "I must have the wrong apartment..."

But then I see Wyatt over the man's shoulder. He sits on his couch, staring at me wide-eyed, face pale. He looks so vulnerable; I want to rush over and wrap my arms around him. The guy who answered the door looks at me, turns over his shoulder, and says, "There's a chick here for one of you." He snaps his gaze back to me. "What's your name?"

"She's here for me." Wyatt appears in the doorway, shoving the man out of the way and reaching for my hand.

He tugs me wordlessly through the apartment and straight into his bedroom. I worry there will be a chorus of teasing, but the entire production is met by awed silence by his roommates, who all seem too tall and too muscular for any of the furniture. I begin to understand why the athletes get their own apartment buildings—everything is bigger in here. They probably have reinforced box springs under their mattresses.

"Fern." Wyatt's voice is gravelly, pained. "You came." He sinks onto the edge of his bed and props his elbows on his knees, cradling his forehead in his palms.

I stand in front of him and rest a hand on his shoulder. "You sounded so upset. Want to tell me what happened?"

He shakes his head and I begin to stroke his shoulder, tracing a fingertip from his ear, down his neck, along the firm swell of muscle. He seems to lean into my touch, so I continue, and eventually, he says, "I feel like I'm putting my entire family at risk, like I'm just some outsider exposing them to trash and scandal."

I sink next to him on the bed and pull him into my arms, resting his head on my shoulder. His body shakes. My mouth is right by his ear as I whisper, "I know they don't feel that way about you. I can tell they'd want to fight this guy alongside you, Wyatt."

His voice is muffled by my shirt. "You haven't even met all of them. The Stag family is intense."

I rub my palms along his back and his arms, just holding him close to me. "From everything you've said, I think they'd get intensely protective of you."

He shakes his head. "That's the problem. They'd drop everything and go wild. And they probably *would* lose endorsements. I can't be the reason any of them lose an opportunity." He draws back to look at me, and his eyes are red and watery. "I'd never forgive myself if my parents got pulled from coaching the national team."

I swallow, looking around for water and not seeing any. I soldier on, voice thick. "What makes you think the team wouldn't rally around them?"

He sighs and pulls back further, reaching for his aunt's book on his nightstand . "This is all about corruption in the national office. My cousin Wes? His girlfriend was the woman who got grabbed and kissed on television. Did you read about that?"

I frown. "It sounds familiar … didn't she start a whole movement? And a clean sweep in the management with a vow to do better by their players?"

Wyatt seems to collapse, like he can't let himself trust that anyone would possibly be on his side in all of this.

"Hey," I tell him, kicking off my shoes and curling up in the bed beside him. I let my hand rest on his face, and he turns toward my palm like a plant angling for sunlight. "I know it's hard to trust people when you're used to going alone. I get it. I was raised by a single mom."

He nods, cuddling closer to me. I've never felt this before, another person relying on me for comfort like this. Let alone a man I find attractive. A man who made me come harder than my expensive (and totally worth the cost) vibrator. I cannot think of Wyatt's bedroom skills right now. He's upset. I knock his baseball hat off his head and bury my fingers in his dark hair instead, gently stroking his head. It's intimate and soothing for both of us. His breath begins to slow, and I can feel him calming down.

"Okay," I tell him. "If this feels like too much, I'll shut up. But you know my friend Thora?"

He nods. "You've mentioned her."

I continue to stroke his hair and tell him about Thora's pre-law adventures and some of the case studies she's described to me. "There's a clinic on campus for legal aid. You see a law student, but it might be more confidential than talking to an official person who might know your family."

Wyatt draws back, frowning up at me. "What good would a student clinic do? I have an agent…"

I nod, bracing myself for him to not want to hear any suggestions. "I just remember Thora talking about petitions for confidential name changes. So, you wouldn't have to advertise it. I'm thinking a student could at least help with that."

Wyatt is quiet for a long time. Just as I worry he's fallen

asleep, he curls a little tighter against me and says, "That could be something."

"It could," I whisper. "I'll get the clinic info from Thora. I can go with you if you want or not—whatever you need."

He looks up at me again, brow furrowed. "Why would you help me like that?"

I shrug. "I like you. We're friends. I think?"

His lips tip up in a small smile. "Yeah, something like that."

He burrows back into my shoulder, and I stroke his hair some more. "What were you going to do tonight? Before you came here, I mean?"

I smile against the top of his head. "I was drinking a milkshake, and then I'd probably read."

His voice is muffled against my shoulder. "What flavor milkshake?"

I laugh and swat at him. "It was hazelnut with little chunks of pretzel. And cherries, of course."

"You're into cherries."

I shrug against him. "I guess so. Sometimes."

I like this cuddly side of him, even as I begin to remember that he is off-limits in this regard. But my urge to help him overpowers my doubts, so I ask, "Want me to read to you since I'm here?"

He pulls back, meeting my eye. "That would be amazing."

"Yeah?" He's unexpectedly enthusiastic, so I disentangle myself from him and crawl toward his bookshelf, studying the spines. "Is that Megan Rapinoe's memoir?"

He stretches out on his back, grinning. "Yeah. I love that one. I know she has a version for adults, but that one's signed."

My jaw drops. "Seriously?" I glance inside the cover, where I see the book is indeed signed and personalized. "Well, we have to read this one, I guess." He nods, and I crawl back to him, sliding under his head so it's on my lap as I open the book. I begin to read, brushing his hair off his forehead with one hand while I recount young Megan's struggles with teachers who didn't like her, with anger she wasn't sure how to contain until she got a soccer ball at her feet.

Each time I glance down, Wyatt's eyes are closed, and I worry he's asleep until he grunts in laughter at the Rapinoe tradition of cleaning out the fridge. "Leftovers don't exist in this apartment, either," he tells me. He waves a hand toward the door. "Those monsters eat everything. Everything."

I close the book and set it aside. "My mom and I eat a pot of soup for like an entire week. It's just us."

He smiles. "Some pros and cons to both those refrigerators, I guess."

I feel warm, happy, and relaxed. I know a crisis for him brought me here, but even if it's forbidden, I'm glad to be right where I am.

"Where were you tonight? Other than milkshakes?"

I glance down at him, and I can't contain the smile that tugs at my mouth. "I was celebrating." He raises his brows, questioning. "I got into my grad program … with funding."

Wyatt draws back, grinning. "That's incredible, Fern. You rock."

A flush builds from my core to the tips of my ears. "It feels pretty damn good."

His gaze heats, and he sits up. "Did you feel all celebrated out? Cuz I can think of some pretty good additions to your milkshake experience."

He licks his lips and snakes a palm onto my hip, tugging me tight against him. I inhale sharply, feeling him fully erect, hard and hot.

I glance down at his sweats, noting the outline bulging between us. "A celebration, hm?"

He nods, splaying his long fingers wider against my butt, digging in and squeezing. "Are you interested in that?"

I close my eyes. "Nobody will know?"

He looks over his shoulder toward his bedroom door. There isn't a sound from outside the door, not even the video game. I have no idea what time it is or how long we've been in here. "They're not going to tell anyone, trust me," Wyatt says with a small smile. "We know better than to blab about who goes in and out of the bedrooms here."

I lick my lips and, rather than prolong the conversation, lean forward to kiss him.

He's familiar and exceptional, warm lips pressing against mine while a tiny moan escapes his throat. I love the feel of it, the sound of his wanting. I rock my hips against him as his hand stays on my ass like all he wants in the world is to feel me pressed into his crotch.

"Fern," he whispers and sucks on my tongue, sending spirals of sparks along my spine. I nibble on his lower lip and explore his mouth with my own tongue, wriggling until my nipples feel the friction against his chest.

I move a hand from his head to his waistband, fingers finding the smooth, taut skin of his abdomen. I trace along the top of his sweats, where his stomach is hairless and firm and so, so warm. In a flurry of elbows and muscular forearms, he whips his shirt over his head and throws it across the room, leaving me with the magnificent sight of his torso. When he rolls onto his back, I can't help but straddle him, pulling off my own shirt and then returning my palms to his chest as he settles me onto his erection.

Even through my jeans, the friction feels perfect. I can tell I'm wet, all the way through my underwear, and Wyatt confirms this when he reaches between my thighs and grins, finding the evidence of my arousal. "Oh, Fern, you gorgeous thing."

I bite my lip and reach behind my back, unclasping my bra. The straps fall from my shoulders, and Wyatt reaches up to slide my hands away. He cups my breasts greedily, squeezing and kneading. "Your body is so fucking incredible," he rasps as I continue wriggling on top of him. In an athletic move I can't comprehend, he sits up without using his hands, and his mouth is back on mine as he continues to touch my boobs, eventually moving to pinch both nipples between his thumbs and forefingers. "Beautiful," he murmurs, never taking his eyes off me.

"That feels so good," I manage to moan, and then I gasp when he dips his head to lick first one nipple and then the other. He leans back, admiring the wet nubs in the dim light from his nightstand. I think about a book Thora gave me once and I stiffen, wondering if Wyatt would be interested in recreating one of the spicy scenes.

He licks and rubs, seeming to enjoy himself immensely as I sit with my hands on his shoulders. Eventually, he looks up, rubbing his cheek against one breast like it's a satin pillow. "What's on your mind, Montgomery?" He arches one eyebrow as I bite my lip. Sensing my hesitation, he straightens. "What's up?"

I take a deep breath and close my eyes, then drop a hand between our bodies, causing him to hiss when my palm rests on his cock. "I was wondering if you'd want to try something …"

CHAPTER 16
WYATT

I BRING my other brow up to match the first at Fern's hesitation. "Beautiful, I'm 100% sure I'm interested in trying whatever's on your mind." The fact that this woman is curious about something in bed has me harder than ever, and I was pretty fucking hard from the moment she put her arms around me, despite being upset and panicking about my family.

Fern has a way of making it feel like things will actually be okay, like there might be a solution out there that doesn't involve me giving up soccer or something like that. She leans in close, lips against my ear. I can feel her breath hot on my cheek as she says, "Would you want to put your cock between my boobs?"

I stiffen, genuinely afraid I'm going to come in my pants at the very thought of burying my dick between Fern's creamy tits. "Holy shit, Fern."

She stiffens. "We don't have to. It was just an idea."

I flip her onto her back in an instant, causing her to yelp. I'm fumbling with my nightstand drawer with one hand, frantically searching for the lube as I yank down my sweat-pants and boxers with my other hand. "Fern. There is nothing in this world I would enjoy more than that. Wow. Found it."

I hold up the bottle of lube, and she frowns. "What's that for?"

"Oh." I shake my head. "Oh, gorgeous, I'm going to slick you up and rub my hands all over you until you're shiny and smooth, and then you're going to hold those awesome boobs together as I grip the headboard and glide in and out."

Her mouth drops open in a sexy oh as I flip open the lid on the bottle of lube. I grin when her hands land on my butt, and I grin even wider as she gasps as the drops of liquid land between her breasts. "Fuuck, Fern," I whisper, watching the rivulets of lube drip along her sternum. When I'm sure there's enough, I get to work spreading it around.

She lies back on my bed, hair all messed up, plush body all soft and warm on my sheets, shining as I lube her up. I set the bottle on the nightstand so I can concentrate, making sure her nipples get some of the action. "Oh, that feels so good, Wyatt," she purrs. Her hands are on my thighs now, everywhere but my erection, which is good because the second she touches me, I know I'll explode. "This is so hot."

I nod. "So, fucking hot. You ready?"

She nods and grips the sides of her boobs. "Oh my god. Fuck, Fern. Jesus." I grip the headboard and slide in, groaning each time I see the head of my cock appear at the top of her cleavage. My breath bursts out of me like I've just played 89 minutes, but I can't lose sight of the goal. I have never felt this turned on in my life ... until Fern gets the idea to stick out her tongue and lick the tip of me the next time I thrust.

She meets my eyes and does it again, and before I can warn her and I can distract myself, I come right there on her chest, splashing my release all over her with a grunt. "Oooh, Wyatt, yes," Fern moans, dabbing a finger in the mess I made. "My god, that was hot." Rather than horrified, Fern seems hornier than ever by my early explosion.

The second I regain consciousness, I yank off her jeans and underwear. I dive down the bed between her thighs as she adjusts her posture, sitting up a bit so she can see what's going on. Fern keeps one finger in the sticky splatter on her boobs and the other hand in my hair as I spread her thighs and lick her. With a few thrusts of my tongue, her head falls back against the headboard. I love watching her come apart like this. She's always so put together, in charge, and confident. It's like I'm the only one who gets to see her this way, disheveled after getting exactly what she asked for.

I move a thumb to her clit, remembering how she liked firm pressure there last time. She tastes like she's desperate for this, and I get hard again, remembering how she was so wet, she seeped through her jeans when we were making out. I tongue her seam, and slide a finger inside feeling her pulsing around me. "That's it, beautiful. You got this." I trace the sensitive skin of her inner thighs, giving her pussy a break until she clamps her knees against my ears. Laughing, I dive back in until I feel the waves and ripples rolling through Fern's body. She drops a forearm over her mouth, stifling her moans as she comes, grunting my name. I hold a finger inside her while she rides it out, and then I kiss my way back up her body, pausing when I get to her chest.

"You are so hot when you come," I tell her.

Lazily, she rolls her face toward mine. "You're just saying that because you're the only one who's seen it."

I frown. "What do you mean?"

She shrugs. "Nobody else has ever been able to do that, Wyatt."

A swell of pride mixes with frustration that she hasn't always gotten what she deserves in bed, which is constant pleasure and satisfaction. I kiss the tip of her nose. "It is my pleasure and my fantasy to see you this way, Fern Montgomery. Fucking look at you."

I glance down at her body, and she does, too, squirming a bit. "I'm a mess."

I nod. "Let's clean you up in the shower."

I do, and then I carry her back to my bed, and she falls asleep beside me, fingers in my hair as I keep a palm on her amazing ass. I know this is a risk for her, that she's got more to lose here than me, and that makes it that much better to know that she's here for me right now. It feels so right like this is exactly where each of us needs to be.

CHAPTER 17
FERN

I WAKE up to the sound of Wyatt's alarm, paired with a fist pounding on his door. "Yo, cuz, we're heading to the weight room. You in?"

Wyatt grunts an affirmative-sounding syllable and rolls to face me. I feel the bed shift, my senses slowly turning on. He plants a kiss on my forehead.

"What time is it?" I don't even want to open my eyes. This can't be when he gets up every day.

"Probably five," he croaks. "But you don't have to rush out of here. Sleep as long as you want and let yourself out." He kisses me on the forehead. It's nice, like how I imagine a boyfriend might wake me up if we lived together. But Wyatt cannot be my boyfriend because he is my student and also because I'm leaving the country in a few months for grad school.

I roll on my back with a groan. "I should go home and shower before class."

I open my eyes to see Wyatt changing into workout gear. His smooth, muscled skin seems to glow in the low light he turned on in the bathroom. By the time I shake the sleep from my eyes, he's brushing his teeth with one hand and pulling on a sock with the other. "Seriously, stay. Nobody will be here. All four of us are going to work out."

Wyatt disappears into the bathroom, and I hear the water running. He appears back by the bed, smelling minty, and kisses my forehead another time. And then he smiles, and he looks so sweet and vulnerable I can't help but swoon right back onto his pillow. "Okay, I'll just close my eyes for a minute."

Wyatt laughs and waves, backing out his door to the grunts of his cousins. I hear low voices and a door close, and then ... I'm alone in Wyatt Moyer's apartment. It feels strange to think of him by the other name, the one he's trying so hard to shed, the one he believes is keeping him from the career he longs for, and the family harmony it sounds like they've fought really hard to build.

I think about how very anxious he is about the whole thing, wondering how long it's been since he talked to a therapist about his past trauma. He mentioned counseling from when he was a child, but it sure sounds like he needs help sorting out his feelings now.

I'm drifting back off to sleep, thinking about how good my body feels after offering him a distraction last night. It was a distraction for me as well and a damn good way to celebrate my acceptance into grad school. Hopefully, Wyatt is right, and nobody in his family will mention me at all, even in passing, to anyone on campus.

Just as I'm convincing myself his cousins don't even know my name and that my secret is safe, I hear a door open. And then I hear Wyatt's bedroom door open. Totally bewildered, I clutch the sheet to my chest as a woman stomps into the room, flicking on the light. Noticing me in the bed, she drops a suitcase on the ground and groans. "Well, shit. This fucking figures."

My cheeks heat in embarrassment and confusion. She exits the room and I hear a lot of commotion out in the living room and kitchen area. Cupboards slam, and music begins to play. I hurry out of bed and get dressed in yesterday's clothes, knowing my hair looks bad as I slept with it wet after rolling around with Wyatt. My cheeks flush remembering how he gently washed me in the shower, how we came together in his bed afterward so tenderly, so slowly. I didn't think I'd have anything left in me after he used his tongue on me earlier, but Wyatt surprised me by coaxing another massive orgasm from my body with his hand while he stroked in and out of my body.

I shake my head and grab my backpack, stepping into the hall.

The woman is sprawled on the sofa with a hand over her eyes. "You don't have to leave. I was just looking for a place to crash in peace. My brother doesn't usually have overnights."

"Brother?" The word is out of my mouth before I can process all the parts of her sentence. Wyatt doesn't bring girls home, or if he does, he doesn't tell his sister about it. Did he mention a sister? Everything is so fuzzy right now.

The woman curls into the sofa, pulling a hooded sweatshirt over her face. Her voice is muffled by the back of the couch. "Look, I'm sure you're delightful, but I am going to pass out until one of them gets back from cardio or whatever."

I stand in the middle of the room, not sure what to do. I'm fully awake now, and I decide I might as well head to campus. I can keep plugging away at the stack of exam papers while I try not to panic that this apparently-exhausted sister of Wyatt's might report our relationship to the university. Which would trigger a cascade of disasters including removing me from the position, taking away the paycheck that comes with it, and probably causing Imperial College to reconsider my fellowship offer.

Nope, I cannot let myself have a staircase of terror thoughts.

I send a message to Wyatt as I wait for the bus to the campus library.

> Met your sister this morning ... I guess she needed a place to crash?

And then, because I know I won't be able to concentrate without asking, I add

> Do I need to worry about her mentioning our sleepover to anyone?

CHAPTER 18
WYATT

THE LAST THING I expect to see when I get back to my apartment after my workout is my sister curled up on my couch. "Birdie? What the hell? Why aren't you in Michigan?"

Our entire family was shocked when my sister begged to move away for high school and play for an elite academy soccer team. Family has always been so important to us, and lord knows we have enough resources here in Pittsburgh to support professional sports aspirations. But Birdie was insistent.

Which does nothing to explain her presence here on my couch. She doesn't respond to my question until I shake her. Gunnar, entering the apartment behind me, pauses by the couch and swats her ass with a pillow. "Birdie Moyer, is that seriously you? Don't you have spring training or some shit?"

She groans and rolls over, her forearm draped across her face. "We're on break, and Mom and Dad are in Texas with the national teams."

I scratch my chin, trying to remember the last time I

talked with my parents. "Wouldn't their house be quieter? A more logical place to get a nap?" She grunts. I glance past her to my open bedroom door, and concern settles icily in my stomach. "Hey, where's, um ... was someone here when you got here?"

Birdie sits up, grinning. "Oh, your lady-friend? She was in your bed when I got here. And then she took off."

"Shit."

Gunnar looks at me, eyes wide. "That chick from last night stayed over? Damn, son." He holds a hand up for a high five.

"Don't be a dick, Gunnar. Come on." I pull my phone out of my sweats and see a few messages from Fern. "I have to check on her."

I head into my room and slam the door, calling Fern's number, but the phone goes right to voicemail. I check the time—it's just past eight, so she wouldn't be in class yet. I scrape a hand down my chin and read her messages. She's worried my sister will, I don't know, call the math dean or something. As if anyone here even knows that Fern is my TA.

I fire off a series of messages to her.

> I'm so sorry about my sister. She's ... a handful.

And then I remember Fern's concerns and add

> She's not going to say anything. I swear. But I do want to follow up with you about the thing you mentioned.

> About the student clinic.

I am about to send another message, like an absolute psycho, when Fern writes back.

FERN MONTGOMERY

> I'll grab the clinic info from Thora ASAP.
> It's probably best if we don't text apart
> from academic matters.

Shit. She's got to be freaking out about her scholarship. I realize that my concern for Fern is overpowering my concern for all the shit with my career and my name and deadbeat Nick. Which should feel like progress, but doesn't. It's strange to be worried about something other than my own crap. And that gets me thinking more about how much these concerns are taking over my life. I try to ignore this and return my thoughts to Fern, who is amazing and so smart and listens to me even when I talk about all my darkness.

I try to respect her boundaries and avoid sending her hourly text updates asking if she heard anything, telling her my family won't say shit to anyone. I want to send her filthy things, telling her how sexy it was the way she came for me, plush thighs wrapped around my waist, amazing ass in my palms as I drove into her. Shit. I don't know if it's hotter that she's sort of forbidden or if she's just fuck-hot, but there's no way I'm concentrating on class this morning with those sorts of memories so fresh in my mind.

When my phone pings with an email, I see it's from Fern and immediately open it. The student law clinic is every Tuesday and Thursday morning, so basically, right the hell now. I change into a nice shirt and slacks—a big change for me since I'm usually wearing athletic stuff—and step into the living room to whistles and jeers from my cousins and my sister, who is now fully awake and playing video games with Odin. "Where the hell are you going?" She sniffs, like I'm wearing ripped clothes and a grease-stained shirt instead of business casual.

"I have a thing," is all I give them. I grab a pea coat from the closet and slip it on, immediately realizing it must belong to Odin because it's fucking huge, but I don't pause to change. I head directly to the clinic, and mercifully, there are only a few people in line ahead of me. One of the clinic workers seems to be the bartender friend Fern mentioned. I frown—I don't know if undergrads are equipped to handle the kind of shit I am here to discuss. But it seems like Thora is mostly handling registration, so I relax a bit.

"Oh," she says, making eyes at me. "It's you! Name, please?"

I hesitate. "Um, that's sort of why I'm here…"

She squints. "I need a name to put on the case file. What's your current legal name?"

I look over my shoulder. "Can I just write it down?" I don't think there is anyone here who might recognize me. I don't have my signature hat pulled over my face, but we're also not really in an area full of undergrads. Everyone mulling about the clinic seems to have shit they're distracted by.

Thora shrugs and slides me her electronic tablet. "We're in the age of modernity. You can type it."

———

I'm sitting outside staring at my official petition for a confidential name change. The law student had access to all the old court records, and it was super uncomfortable rereading those documents. I had sort of suppressed the court appearances from when I would have to go to his house for visitation, and he would refuse to feed me if I cried or made noise, and Mom kept trying to change the custody order.

I'm a little twitchy remembering all the incidents my mom never found out about because the police never got involved. But the supervising lawyer at the clinic today said we didn't even need to get into all that because there was enough paperwork from custody court paired with the threatening texts.

I was embarrassed to tell them that I initiated contact, but I think the law school folks understand what it's like to hope your parents will raise you.

I gave them a check that was less than a tank of gas in my Range Rover, and they're going to file all this stuff for me with the magistrate.

All I want to do is call Fern and thank her, properly. But she's spooked about my sister. Fern and I never seem to get enough time alone. I realize I have just the way to overcome that obstacle, in a place where Fern won't worry about us being seen or anyone reporting our relationship to her boss.

I look at my watch. I have no idea what her schedule is like on Tuesdays, but I do know she has a mailbox in the math department. I form a plan and scrawl a note to her on the back of the law clinic flyer Thora handed me outlining their services and fees.

As I make my way to the math building, I hope I run into Fern in person, but I don't hold out much hope of that. I slip the folded flyer into the pigeonhole above her name and head home to prepare while I wait for her response.

CHAPTER 19
FERN

"MS. MONTGOMERY, can I speak to you for a moment?" Professor Yoon summons me from the cubicle where I'm grading papers near their office.

"Sure. What's up?" I sink into the seat opposite their desk, cringing a little at how informally I just answered them. They always seem so serious and busy. I can't get a read on them.

They set down a stack of papers and glance at me over the top of their glasses. "I heard about your acceptance to Imperial College. Congratulations." They don't smile when they say this so I'm not sure how to respond.

"Thank you?" My voice tilts up at the end of my sentence. "It's a huge honor."

Professor Yoon takes off their glasses and folds their fingers together. "It's an honor for us as well, to have prepared a student for such a prestigious program. I will be following your career with interest." I can't quite tell, but it almost seems like they smile, so I relax a bit and let out a huge breath. They pick up one of the papers from their desk. "I'm told you are avoiding grading the word problems on the exam?"

My cheeks flush. Have the other teaching assistants been talking about me? My heart races a bit. "Um, well, some of the students' answers have seemed partially correct and I wasn't sure how to give credit for those."

Professor Yoon chews on one of the stems of their glasses. "I do not typically award partial credit. Math is a very precise endeavor, as you know." I nod. They sigh. "It occurs to me that you have not had the benefit of an orientation. The other teaching assistants get a bit of guidance when they arrive for graduate school. Have there been other gaps preventing you from completing your work?"

My eyebrows shoot up. There have been so many gaps I don't even know where to begin, but it won't do me any favors to ask them to start at the beginning. Especially since we're a month into the semester at this point. I clear my throat. "Um, not that I can think of? But I might not know what I don't know… my recitation grades are still just pass-fail based on attendance, right?" They nod. I think of Wyatt, of how I should have mentioned a prior relationship with him a long, long time ago, but now that ship has sailed halfway to London. "I'm good," I stammer. "I'm enjoying learning the ropes."

Now Professor Yoon actually smiles. "You won't need ropes for long. You won't even have the burden of teaching your first year in England."

I am surprised to learn they think of teaching as a burden. I think about how much I enjoy breaking down the concepts with my recitation students and how it helps my own thinking for my work when I have to explain basic concepts. I shrug. "It's a great scholarship."

They nod. "Well, back to it." They slide me the pile of

exams, and I head back to the cubicle to re-do them. Right or wrong. No gray area for Professor Yoon. I need to keep that in mind.

I pass the row of mailboxes on my way and see that there is something in mine. I grab the slip of paper and see that it's a flyer from the student law clinic.

Wyatt.

I look over my shoulder, which is ridiculous because I would surely hear if there were someone else in the hall. Seeing no one, I unfold the paper and see a handwritten note from him on the back of the form.

Sorry again about my sister. Thanks again for the law clinic advice. I have so much to tell you. Let me take you somewhere we can talk? Say yes. Call me.

I sink back into my seat in the cubicle, staring at the mountain of exam papers, thinking about my own course-work as well as lesson plans for Friday's recitation. What does he even mean, take me somewhere?

I grade papers for another hour, trying to get as many done as I can, which is a little easier now that I'm not giving anyone room for doubt if they got the answer wrong but the approach correct … it's not a policy I would choose, but it's not my call.

What is my call, is the hushed conversation I have with Wyatt from the 23rd floor, where nobody is around because I checked. Twice.

"Hey," he answered. "You got my note?"

"I did," I whisper, which I realize might make me seem even more suspicious if someone shows up. I remind myself that nobody would have any idea who I'm talking to as long as I don't use his name. "What did you mean?"

I can practically hear him smiling, which is unusual for him. "My family has a house in the mountains, right on the ski resort in Hidden Valley. Let me take you there?"

I puff out a laugh. "I don't ski. Is there even snow?" Our winters have been incredibly mild lately.

He scoffs. "We wouldn't be going there to ski, Fern. Although I can teach you if you want." I frown. He continues. "I'd cook for you. And there's a hot tub."

A vision of Wyatt shirtless in bubbly water is impossible to tamp down in my mind. Fuck, that sounds amazing. "When would we even do something like that?"

"Any time. Nobody uses that place during the week. Do I remember that you only have one class on Thursday? We could go Wednesday afternoon, skip your class, get back in time for you to be my teacher Friday ... "

I am positive my entire face and neck are bright red at this point. Two entire nights in a mountain cabin with Wyatt Moyer sounds like something from a romance novel. One of the books where I got my idea for that thing we did the other night. "I can hear you breathing hard, Fern." Wyatt's voice teases me. "I'm sure you've never skipped a class before in your life, and you probably know all the material."

I bite my lip. My Thursday class this semester is the art history class I saved for this year because it's pure enjoyment. It doesn't even count toward my degree, although I'm using it as an elective. The professor is one of those people who gets me to see the world differently and think about art not just as a bonus but as an important part of being human. "I don't know if I *want* to miss my Thursday class," I admit.

"Hm. Well, think about it. I can make it worth your while. Over and over again … in the hot tub. On the counter. On the rug by the fire…"

"Okay, okay. Wow."

"Are you blushing, Fern? I wish I could see. Snap a picture."

I hear someone come up the stairwell and turn to see a red-faced student huffing and puffing a bit. Hopefully, they see me in a similar state and assume I also took the stairs up here. "You have to stop talking that way."

"Meet me at my apartment tomorrow?"

I bite my lip. "What do I even bring?"

Wyatt laughs. "Strip of condoms and a bottle of lube?"

"Wyatt!" I swear I'm going to pass out if he keeps talking this way.

He laughs again. "Just comfortable clothes. There are sheets and towels at the house. I'll take care of all the food and everything. Including you …"

———

We hang up, and I immediately call Thora, who texts me that she picked up a bartending shift and can't talk. I feel this counts as an emergency, so I make my way to the bar on Forbes Avenue, where I first met Wyatt Moyer on New Year's Eve.

Thora is slinging bowls of soup and pints of dark beer to the lunch crowd, and I make my way up to the bar, grabbing a stool at the far end, hopefully out of earshot of … well, everyone.

Thora's brow furrows when she sees me, and she slides a menu my way along the bar. "What are you doing here? You never spend money."

I lean forward. "I have to tell you something."

She bites her lip. "Bowl of soup?"

I glance at the prices on the menu. "Cup of soup."

She nods and disappears, serves a bunch of food and drink to some other patrons, and makes her way back to me, where she starts rinsing glasses. "What happened?"

I tell her about my chat with Professor Yoon and Wyatt's indecent proposal. She grins. "I did see him at the clinic. He left there pretty happy. He had some weird thing about his name?"

I wave a hand. "That's not our business. The point is he wants to …" I don't even know how to describe what he seems to be offering.

She leans across the bar and takes a bite of my soup. "He wants to sex you up in a fancy-ass ski chalet where nobody is going to interrupt you."

"I'm sure it's not a chalet."

Thora arches a brow. "You really haven't looked up his family at all? They're, like, super famous Pittsburgh royalty."

I frown at her. "I had no idea."

She nods. "I've been doing a little stalking action on his cousin Odin, arguably the hottest Stag."

I recoil. "Odin? He's …" obnoxious … loud … not Wyatt … I'm not sure how to finish that sentence.

Thora pats the bar. "He's in my argument class. I'm supposed to work with him on the next paper."

I laugh. "Well, you'll like that. He's an athlete so you can probably–"

"Boss him around? Take over the project entirely." She beams. "You know me so well." A bell rings from the kitchen, and Thora rushes off to grab another order, shouting over her shoulder. "It's okay if you're smitten with Wyatt. There are way more sexy dudes in his family, though, for the rest of us. And you should definitely go to the *Winter Palace*. Do it for the rest of us, toiling away behind the bar." She leans back and presses the back of her hand to her face like a fainting Victorian woman.

I roll my eyes at her and finish my soup.

CHAPTER 20

FERN

I JUMP when my mom rests her hand on my back. And then I groan. "What time is it?"

Mom pulls up the seat next to mine. "It's almost six. I just got home. Have you been here all day?"

My back aches, and I stand, trying to stretch as I simultaneously blink to wet my dried-out eyeballs. "I have all this grading to get done for Professor Yoon."

"Mm." Mom frowns at the stack. "I thought you had a whole week for those?"

I bite my lip. I've already decided to go with Wyatt. I hate missing my class, but I also rarely do anything spontaneous. I never do anything decadent. "I'm, um, going out of town for a few days this week. With a friend."

Mom arches a brow. "A friend who is *not* Thora?"

I laugh because Mom knows as well as I do that Thora and I are never going to ditch class and work mid-week to go adventuring. At least not while we're undergrads. Who knows what will happen when she's a Rhodes Scholar and I'm in "fancy math school," as she calls it. "A friend who is not Thora." I shrug, not wanting to upset my mother or give her all the sordid details. "I'm trying to live a little. Be young. What are you always telling me?"

"Hm. Mid-week? What about class?"

I sit back down next to Mom. I glance at my stack of papers—only a few left. "I've never missed a single art history class, and everyone gets one freebie with no penalty. And I'll be back before my math recitation on Friday. And as you can see—" I point at the stack. "—I'm well ahead of the curve with my work for that gig." I lean my head on Mom's shoulder. "Think of it like the spring break I never took."

Mom sighs and kisses the top of my head. "You're right. I trust you. You're always responsible, and you're older than I was when I had you."

I frown at her. "You don't sound so certain."

"Well, you're not giving me many details." We both laugh and Mom gets up, opens the fridge, and we set to cooking dinner together, my stack of papers forgotten for the time being. As I stir and chop, I think about how many people seem capable of no-string flings. This trip with Wyatt doesn't have to mean anything. I can let him ravish me away from the prying eyes of soccer fans on campus and anyone who might put my TA position in jeopardy.

This can be a delicious cherry on top of my undergraduate career before I head off to … well, frankly, more of the same hard work in graduate school. Just on a different continent with different things to see on weekends. From what I've read, Imperial College takes graduate students on weekend excursions to the moors and day trips to Stonehenge. I feel a little giddy thinking about a theoretical advanced math discussion about Stonehenge with a bunch of like-minded students.

And I'll be a train ride away from Paris! The idea of seeing the Eiffel Tower when I've never even seen the Statue of Liberty is a bit surreal. Mom heads to her room after dinner, and I finish grading, typing in the last of the grades, and packing up the papers to drop off with Professor Yoon first thing in the morning. Before I try to sleep, I pack my ratty old swimsuit, which will have to do, along with my best sensible underwear, dark jeans, and a few tops like the one I had on New Year's Eve when Wyatt apparently fell hard for my rack.

In the end, I don't get much sleep at all, anticipating my big sordid adventure. But when Wyatt picks me up outside the math department, I forget all about being tired. I climb into his black SUV, sink into the leather seats, and smile as he points the car east and heads toward the mountains.

"Tell me about this place," I insist as he merges onto the highway and calmly enters tunnel traffic.

Wyatt grins, a wide smile I'm not used to seeing on his face. "My dad and his brothers all went in on it when Uncle Tim turned 40. It's nice having a place big enough for all of us."

I lean one elbow on the window and rest my head on my hand. "When you say all of us ... how many is that, exactly?"

My whole family is me and Mom, so I'm fully unprepared when Wyatt spits out the number 19. My jaw drops as he ticks off aunts, uncles, and cousins. "Oh," Wyatt adds. "There's also Grand and Lolly. Dad's mom, Lolly, married my mom's friend Patty—my Grand." He shrugs. "So, 21 if they come to stay when we're there." He scratches his chin. "Wes is feeling pretty permanent about his girl, but we haven't all been together since he's been with Cara. I bet it'll be 22 of us for Christmas."

I try not to imagine making it 23, try not to think about being in this fantasy castle bursting with family … with Wyatt.

He tells me the place has an indoor soccer field, a theater room, a pool *and* a hot tub, and enough bunk beds for an entire soccer team. "The best part is the big table, though," Wyatt adds. "It's really, really nice when we all sit together eating amazing food Aunt Alice makes. She's the chef. I think I told you about her."

I smile at him. "You sound really happy when you talk about your family."

He frowns at this. "Yeah." He sighs. "I've been caught up in this shit with my bio dad. Ever since he started contacting me … making weird threats. It's been heavy. I guess I get nostalgic for big Stag getaway weekends."

As Wyatt exits the turnpike, the big buildings of the city give way to rolling hills and frosty trees. "I guess it really is colder up here in the mountains."

He nods. "Yeah. I told you, it's an escape to a different world." We drive along, and I wonder if I should ask him about his progress with the name petition, but I decide it's too soon for anything to have happened, even if he was able to pay to fast-track things.

Before I can fret about it too long, Wyatt turns into Hidden Valley Ski Resort and points up the hill. "We're headed up there, right on the slope."

My eyes widen. "Won't people *see* the house if it's on the slope?"

He shrugs. "Sometimes people on the lift can see you if

you're in the hot tub during the day. But we'll be very secluded tonight, Fern. I promise."

His last word carries so much heat that I shiver, so far gone my lust overtakes all my worries about being seen by … exactly who do I think is looking at me from the ski slopes? Certainly, not anyone who is in the position to tattle on me to the math department about making out with a student in a foggy hot tub on a rich family's deck.

"Here we are," he says, pulling into the driveway to a massive house with a sloped roof and multi-story windows overlooking the forest.

"Wow," is all I can muster, and when I look to my side, Wyatt is staring at me.

"Yeah," he says, not looking away from my face. "Wow."

CHAPTER 21
WYATT

I CARRY the cooler and grocery bags inside while Fern drops her bag and stares around the great room. Not gonna lie, the first view of this place is always spectacular. By the time I make a second trip in from the car, she's figured out the remote for the fireplace and turned on the recessed lights above the massive wooden table.

I decide right there in the doorway that I'm going to spread her out on that table and make her come. My own private feast. I drop the last grocery bag on the counter and walk up behind her, looping my arms around her waist as she stares out the window. I kiss the side of her neck, feeling her melt into me. "Want a tour?"

She shakes her head. "I just want to stand here for a bit, if that's okay."

"Whatever you want." I nuzzle at her, letting my hands trace across her soft belly, growing hard as she sighs and stares at the beauty of the Laurel Highlands. She rests her head back against my shoulder, and I startle, realizing how fucking good it feels to just hold her this way. I have no worries here, no responsibilities.

I don't even have cell reception to worry if my agent is going to call, or my new lawyer. Until I connect to the household Wi-Fi, I'm in my own little world with Fern Montgomery. I reach for her hand. "Come on." I give it a tug. "Let me show you our room."

———

I walk Fern down the hall, past the bunk room, up the stairs, and into my parents' bedroom. My dad and each of his brothers have a room with a king-sized bed, and there's a queen suite in the basement for Grand and Lolly. But there's no way I can achieve what I need to with Fern in a bunk bed, so I take her into the first room at the top of the stairs.

She's in my arms in a flash, mouth sealed against mine as I flick on the light and then hoist her into my arms. She wraps those thighs around me as I walk toward the bed, and when I finally sink on top of her, it's like the world exhales.

"Wyatt." Fern's voice is in my ear, her breath hot on my skin. I feel the heat between her legs as she keeps them wrapped around my waist.

"You look so good here with me," I tell her, admiring the flush in her cheeks before I tug her shirt up and over her head. "God, your body is so luscious." She smiles as I kneel above her, palming her boobs.

Fern tugs at my shirt, struggling to sit up, so I help her out and pull it off with one hand behind my neck. And then we are skin to skin, moaning into each other's mouths. I slide down her body to lick at her nipples, and she drags her fingernails down my chest.

"I thought this was going to happen in the hot tub,"

she whispers, biting my trap muscle and then sucking the spot where her teeth pinched me.

"Mmm," I lick each nipple and then thumb the wet peaks. "We can do that after. To recover."

Fern opens her jeans and slides them down her hips. I do the same with my pants until we're both fully naked on top of the covers. "Shit," I freeze. "I left the condoms downstairs in my bag."

Fern pouts. "You better hurry and get them. You can't leave me like this, Wyatt." She spreads out on the blanket and drops a hand between her legs.

"Fuuck, Fern. Do not move." I sprint down to the doorway and grab my entire bag, taking the steps three at a time as I rush back to find her … not in the same position at all. No. Fern has rolled onto her stomach, the glory of her naked ass on display for me as her dark hair spills over one shoulder and she presses up into some sort of yoga cobra pose that pushes her tits together.

I almost choke on my tongue. "My god, Fern. Look at you." I throw the bag onto the bed and dive on top of her, feeling the swell of her ass against my dick, which is harder than I ever thought possible.

Her voice is husky when she says, "Mm, you're so warm." She turns her head to the side, and I kiss her as I fuss with the bag with one hand. Finding the condom, I yank it on as quickly as I can and then nudge her thighs open, settling between them.

"I want to take you like this," I whisper into her ear. "All spread out for me, that incredible ass where I can see it. Oh, my, you *are* wet." My fingers spread her open, finding her pulsing and hot and so soft.

"Wyatt!" Her cry is a gasp as I pull my hand out from her body. "Oh god, I need…"

"Mm, I know what you need." I kiss her shoulder and line myself up behind her, one palm on her ass and one on the base of my cock as I notch up and start to push inside. The sight of her like this, spread around me, soft and perfect, almost has me losing myself before I even finish a stroke.

"That's it," I tell her as she buries her face in her hands, disappearing behind a curtain of hair. "Look how easily you take me, gorgeous."

And she does. Fern swallows me inside, pulsing and hot around me. "Wyatt, it feels so good like this." She presses her forearms into the bed and shifts her hips back, moving to meet me as I start to thrust inside her. I let her take all of my weight, leaning over her and sucking on her shoulder as my hands search for her breasts. "Oh," she moans. "Oh, do that some more." I pinch her nipples as I grind into her, and she tilts her hips.

"Fuck, Fern, can you get up on your knees? I need to touch you, beautiful." She lifts herself up, giving me access to her clit as I snake an arm around her hip. I band the other across her chest and, feeling inspired, pull her upright so we're both on our knees. Fern grips the headboard with both hands, pinned against me as I flick her nipples and knead her clit, all the while thrusting inside her and trying not to come until I hear her shrieking and feel her pulse around me.

And then we're both coming, shaking, collapsing in a fit of giggles and released tension, curled together on the bed in a sweaty, sated knot.

CHAPTER 22
WYATT

WHEN I FINALLY TUCK FERN INTO a fluffy towel and tug her out back to the hot tub, a bottle of white wine and two glasses between the fingers of my left hand, she's already sex-drunk and utterly relaxed.

And then she sees the sky full of stars, away from the lights of the city, sparkling above the treeline as the steam from the hot tub swirls upward. "Climb on in," I tell her, gesturing for her towel, which I hang on a peg by the hot tub along with my own. I've never been naked in my family's hot tub before, never brought a woman here to curl against my chest with a drink under the stars. "This is amazing," I whisper.

Fern turns her head, incredulous. "Wyatt. I know. But surely you're used to it by now?"

I shake my head. "How could I ever get used to this? Look at you." I squeeze her waist before turning to open the wine and pour us each a glass. I set the bottle on the shelf behind the headrest in the corner of the hot tub, where the jets are cranking.

"Well," she blows her hair away from her face and accepts a glass of wine. "Look at you. And look around."

I nod. "We are both incredible, and the scenery is pretty okay." Fern throws her head back, laughing, and takes a sip of her drink.

She rests her head sleepily against my shoulder. "I don't think I'm going to be able to do much else tonight after all that."

"You don't want to do *all that* again?" Just the thought of it has my dick twitching against her back, but I guess she doesn't notice it with the water jets because Fern sighs into her wine glass.

"I really don't think I can handle that again."

"I'm up for the challenge if you are." I grin and squeeze her hand, and we both sip and stare at the stars.

Fern turns to me, arms around my neck, facing me in the dark water. "I should tell you something."

I nod. "I've told you plenty of things."

Fern smiles and runs her fingers through my hair in that way I love so much. "You're the only person I've been with. Like that I mean."

I frown. "Like what?"

She shrugs. "Like, put their penis inside my vagina." Another smile, and she presses a kiss on my forehead. "It was something I really *really* wanted to do on New Year's, and I'm glad it was you because it was incredible."

I'm not sure what to say in response to that, so I just stare at her a few beats. I set my wine glass on the shelf and pull her tighter against me. "Thank you," I whisper. "For trusting me with that. I'm … touched? I don't know what word to use."

"Don't let it go to your head," she says with a laugh, reaching past me to get my wine glass and handing it to me again. "I just didn't want you to be the only one confessing things about your identity."

"I appreciate that." I settle back against the headrest, appreciating how intimate it is here with her, curled up like this, but also so natural and really fucking nice.

The jets shut off after twenty minutes, reminding me that I need to keep Fern hydrated and probably fed if I want to make good on my promise to ply her with orgasms. I hop out of the tub and quickly wrap my towel around my waist, opening hers up for her to step in as she gingerly climbs down the steps.

"It's a lot nicer getting in than getting out." Her teeth chatter as I grab the wine, flip the lid back on the hot tub, and run inside, where I grab a container from the cooler and slide it into the oven.

By the time I've heated up our meal, I've thoroughly warmed Fern up by the fireplace. After we eat, I warm her up again in bed and we fall asleep in each other's arms, as if we can stay this way.

As if we're both not on the brink of leaving the country, facing potential scandal, or technically forbidden from being together. None of that seems to matter as I pull her tighter against my chest, one palm on her butt and her palm above my heart.

CHAPTER 23
FERN

I WAKE up to the smell of coffee. I open my eyes to find Wyatt kneeling by the bed, holding a steaming white mug. He's smiling, looking so content and relaxed.

A lazy smile tugs at my own lips as I work to sit up in bed. I realize I'm still naked and a little bit sore. But it's wonderful. He's shirtless, too, and climbs back in bed beside me, a mug of his own in his hand. "Morning, beautiful."

He clinks his mug against mine and cuddles against my side. And this might be the best way I've ever woken up in my entire life. I'm delightfully warm and comfortable. I sip at the coffee, which has the perfect amount of milk and nothing else.

He kisses my neck in between sips and feeling content; I do the same. Until we're tangled together, mugs forgotten, making out like morning breath doesn't matter. Despite the ache between my legs, I'm desperate for friction yet again, and I move to straddle Wyatt in the bed. Until he grips my wrist. "There's something I really want to do with you."

I furrow my brow and look at him, brushing my hair back from my eyes. "Something we didn't already do last night?"

Wyatt grins wickedly and scoops me into the air. Both of us naked, he sprints down the stairs as if I weigh nothing at all, and I yelp as he begins to lower me onto the wooden table by the massive windows overlooking the ski slopes.

I glance to my side, seeing the chair lift in operation on the mountain. "Wyatt!" I drop a hand to cover my breast even as he spreads my legs open, positioning me at the end of the table. "What are you doing?"

He sinks to the floor, his long legs kneeling on the wood, torso aligned with my thighs. "They can't see in, Fern. Tinted windows."

I feel his palms on my legs and bite my lip, studying the glass. "It doesn't look tinted—oh!"

He starts licking me, long, slow strokes of his warm tongue. He gently places one thigh and then the other over his shoulders so I'm surrounding his head as he burrows between my legs. There's nothing for me to do but run my fingers through his messy hair and relax into the sensation.

Wyatt licks me like I'm a dessert. Here, in this mansion on the mountain, he makes me feel like I'm the most precious, necessary thing he ever dreamed of. It goes on for what feels like ages until I'm moaning his name and arching my back, waves of pleasure crashing around me. Every time I open my eyes, I see Wyatt's face, his eyes dark with lust and his lips glistening with my own moisture. It's filthy and wonderful, and I come, shouting his name until it echoes off the pristine walls.

After, he carries me back up to bed, where our coffee is waiting. And it's almost like it never happened, except I'm fully sated, and he's hard as stone, one hand lazily stroking himself while he drinks his coffee and stares at me.

I set my mug back on the nightstand and turn to face him. "That was pretty special, you know."

He grins. "I've been dreaming of doing that." I stare down at his crotch, loving the way his hand looks fondling his length.

I run a hand along his chest. "What exactly do you do when you dream of that?"

He arches a brow, setting his empty mug on his nightstand. "I think you know what I do, Fern."

I climb over him, one leg on either side of his, but settle myself midway down his thighs, not touching him where he's glistening and leaking. I like the feel of his hairy legs against my smooth ones. "I want you to tell me. And show me." I bite my lip, placing my hands on his shoulders. He sucks in a breath and moves his hand more rapidly along his cock.

"I touch myself until I come," he whispers, eyes closed. And then his eyes fly wide, staring at my body, my face.

"I want to see," I tell him, and I really, really do want that. I want to see his head thrown back in ecstasy, hot ropes of release splattering his rock-hard abs. "Show me, Wyatt. Show me what you do when you think about eating me out on your dining table. Show me how it turns you on to make me come so hard."

"Fuck, Fern." His hand flies along his dick, his other flailing through my hair, finding purchase, tugging. It stings, electrifying. We lock eyes, and I watch his face contort as he gets closer to the edge. I can see why it turns him on so much to go down on me. Inspired, feeling brave, I scoot backward and out of his grasp. I stick out my tongue and taste the tip of him, a salty burst of moisture on my tongue. "Oh, gorgeous, you don't have to. I wanted to make today about you …"

Wyatt is panting like he's just finished a match. I place a hand on his thigh, the other on top of his own hand, grasping his erection. "This is about me," I whisper.

And it's true. As I slide my mouth onto him, I can feel the power I have in this moment. I can feel his surrender, the awe and appreciation he's experiencing alongside the evident pleasure. I'm delighted to learn I can draw groans and grunts from Wyatt's mouth as I lick and suck, tease and kiss. His hand drops away, cupping my chin. When I glance up at him, with several inches of him in my mouth, his eyes fly wide, and his head drops back. Wyatt emits a bellow and comes forcefully into my mouth. I pull off, licking at the drops of his pleasure but watching greedily as more white ropes spray up onto his abs. It's filthy and just what I wanted to see.

When I reach out to dab a finger in the mess and then taste that, too, Wyatt seems to actually pass out.

———

Hours later, or maybe it's days or months … we're finally dressed, cuddling in the kitchen while he heats up some sort of breakfast casserole he brought in the giant cooler of delights. I can't stop kissing him and giggling, touching him as we wait to eat. It's like any millimeter of space between us is far too much after what we just shared.

And then I hear a car door slam, the sound of women laughing. I stiffen. Wyatt hasn't heard yet. He's nibbling at my chin when the front door of the house opens to reveal a woman with a salt-and-pepper ponytail flanked by an older woman with a short bob and ... my art history professor.

The three of them stop laughing and stare at us, the older two women tittering with laughter and the younger one dropping her hands to her hips. "Wyatt Henry De Luca! What the hell are you doing here?"

CHAPTER 24

WYATT

"FERN, WAIT!" She ducked out of my arms and sprinted up the stairs when my fucking mother barged into the house. I'm torn between wanting to run after Fern and tell her everything will be okay, and facing the apparent repercussions of bringing her here without checking in with my family that they weren't using the place.

Mom stands in my way, hands on her hips, while Grand and Lolly laugh hysterically behind her. "Wyatt Henry De Luca," she repeats. And that does it.

"Do not use that name, Mom. I've asked you so many times."

She shakes her head, appalled. "That's your response right now? An irritation about semantics?"

"It's not a fucking irritation. God, you know how much I hate any connection to that name. It makes me sick." I try to shove past her after Fern, but she places a hand on my shoulder.

Mom's face softens. "Wyatt, baby. We need to talk. Your friend is okay. Nobody is going to chase her down." I grit my teeth, wondering if Fern is spooked enough to jump out the window upstairs and ski to freedom. I decide she's not that foolish and I follow Mom over to the sofa, thankful she didn't head for the wooden table I still need to clean off.

"I think I know her," Grand says, glancing up the stairs where Fern disappeared. "Is she a student? She is. She's one of *my* students." Grand laughs, joining us on the couch. "Imagine that!"

"Glad you find this so amusing," Mom snorts. "Wyatt, what are you doing here? You know there's a schedule for the ski house."

This is the first I've heard of a schedule, but it shouldn't surprise me, knowing my family. I wonder how many times this happens—someone bringing a romantic partner out here only to be thwarted by another Stag looking to relax in peace and quiet. I glare at my mom. "I thought you were in Texas with the national team."

She sneers. "That was days ago. This is my relaxing wind-down after our loss. Which you'd know if you checked the AirTable your uncle set up."

Lolly holds up her phone. "It's an app, dear. See? Your dad is coming out tomorrow, and we think maybe Birdie can join us on Saturday!"

I drag a hand down my chin, and then the oven timer scares the shit out of all of us. "That's the casserole," I mutter. I jump up to pull it out of the oven before it burns when a thought occurs to me. "Why didn't Aunt Alice say anything if she knew you guys were coming? She made me all this food … "

Mom arches a brow. "You told your aunt you were having a …" Mom bites her lip. "Romantic getaway? Here?"

"Well." I stare at the French toast mixture. "Not exactly. But I asked her what food would be good for a few days away with someone I'm trying to impress and —" I end my sentence abruptly when Fern appears at the stairs with her bag, eyes red like she's been crying. "Hey," I shout, rushing over to her. "You don't need to leave. I told you I'd take care of you."

Fern tries to hide her face, and I put together what Grand just said. She's one of Grand's students. I'm one of Fern's students. Fuck.

Grand stands and reaches for a plate, helping herself to some of the casserole. "I think we should all sit down and eat and have a conversation." She starts walking toward the table.

"No!" Fern and I shout together before my grandma can sit at the head of the table.

Grand arches a brow and pivots toward the island, lowering herself into one of the bar chairs. She pats one next to her and looks at Fern. "Have a seat, Ms. Montgomery."

I stand frozen as Fern sinks into the chair next to Grand. Lolly mutters something about running to town for coffee, and Mom stares at all of them like she can't tell what's going on.

Finally, Mom says, "Well, Wyatt, introduce us." She crosses her arms over her chest, adopting a stance I've seen her take while bossing around professional athletes on the soccer field.

I lick my lips. "Mom, I mean Lucy Moyer … this is Fern Montgomery. Fern, this is my mom, and I guess you know my Grand … what are the odds of that?"

Fern looks pale and Grand slides her a glass of orange juice she procured from my cooler. Smiling, Grand reaches for the champagne I had chilling in there alongside it. "You were doing it up right, Wyatt. Mimosas are a great idea, I think. Lucy?" Mom shakes her head.

Still looking pale, Fern sips at her drink. "Cheers," Grand says, holding up her flute. She smacks her lips and pats Fern on the arm. "Fern—can I call you Fern when we're not in class?" Fern nods. Grand smiles. "Fern, I think it's great that you and Wyatt are having a good time together. My wife Holly will be the first to tell you I'd forget about that scheduling app for the house, too. There's plenty of room for all of us here if you two want to stay."

I groan and Mom huffs. She mutters something under her breath about disinfectant and I flush, knowing there are a few surfaces here I planned to scrub before we left. Grand squeezes Fern's hand. "And isn't it interesting that you're here during our class time, and I'm here, too? I guess we both played hooky today." Grand smiles, fussing with one of her earrings. She looks over at my mom and asks, "Am I remembering that you were trying to keep things quiet when you started dating Hawk? That was right after that terrible incident with the hot car." Grand winces and looks over at me.

I remember when I met her—when she used a brick to smash the window in my father's car to get me out of the heat, saving me from suffocating. The weight of the memory washes over me in nauseating waves and I sink into the chair on the other side of Grand. Mom swallows and reaches for a champagne flute. "Hopefully that was a very different circumstance," Mom says, sparing a small smile for Fern. "I'm sorry we didn't get to meet each other properly. Fern, is it?" Now Mom's smile is genuine. "I've never gotten to meet one of Wyatt's girlfriends before."

Fern's eyes widen. "Oh, it's not...I'm moving..."

I clear my throat. "We're just hanging out for now, Mom." Realizing I can change the subject to much easier material, I add, "Fern got accepted into a PhD program in London."

Grand claps her on the back. "That's wonderful. Is it related to math? You've been so interested in that fractal article."

Fern nods and starts talking about algebraic geometry, which keeps them all from asking about my contract, my father, my mess and my forbidden entanglement with my TA. By the time Lolly gets back from the store, the four of us have finished all but one slice of the breakfast casserole and I've managed to spray the table clean while scrubbing up the island from our meal.

I get the sense Fern doesn't want to actually finish out our second night here—not with my mother and grand-mothers—so I hurry upstairs to change the bed linens. I come down to find Fern white-faced while my grand-mother promises not to mention her to Professor Yoon, the big shot math guy in charge of Fern's job. Grand waves a finger in the air. "I know Jae-won from the LGBTQ faculty summit. We go way back. But they don't need to know we were both skipping class today." Grand meets my eye and I know I'm going to have a lot to discuss with her once I get Fern back home.

CHAPTER 25
FERN

I CAN'T FIND words to talk to Wyatt in the car as he drives me back to Pittsburgh. I pick at my cuticles while he navigates the twisting roads until I guess he can't take the silence anymore and yells, "I can't believe my fucking mom and grandmas walked into my sexy vacation."

I turn and stare, biting back a laugh. "Sexy vacation?"

He grins. "Was it not sexy?" Wyatt waggles his eyebrows, and I relax a bit.

I sigh. "It was very sexy. But very dangerous, apparently. Your grandma is my professor."

Wyatt scratches his chin. He hasn't shaved, and the dark stubble coming in looks really good on him. It makes him look like a pirate. "My Grand isn't going to tell anyone about us, you know. That's not how she rolls."

I burrow deeper into the passenger seat. "It's not a conscious thing always, though. It's a comment at a staff meeting or a knowing glance my way when Professor Yoon can see … there are a million reasons this was a terrible idea, and I probably should have just told my advisor about you back in January, and now it's way too late for that. I'm really worried that everything I've worked for is going to sink into a pit of farts."

Wyatt waits for a beat after my explosion of anxiety, finally saying, "Does it feel better to get all that out? That was a lot ... "

I don't look at him. "It was a lot, and no. It doesn't feel better." Except it kind of does. Verbalizing all of that makes it sound a little less ... daunting. What if I went to Professor Yoon and told them about Wyatt? Would they write a letter to Imperial College? Would they withhold my transcript? Unlikely. But the possibility is still there.

Wyatt drives through the Squirrel Hill Tunnel, and we are nearly back in my neighborhood. If he was an ordinary boyfriend, I'd have him walk up and say hello to my mother. But he's not my boyfriend, and we're coming back early from an illicit mid-week tryst. My mother is at work. "Wyatt." I look at him as he pulls up along the curb outside my apartment building. "We can't do this again."

He nods. "Trust me, I'm figuring out the calendar app as soon as I drop you off."

I shake my head. "No, I mean, we can't do this." I gesture back and forth between us. "We need to maintain a professional relationship, and that's it."

He frowns. "We are way past all of that, Fern. You know I'm not going to say a damn thing, and I'm not going to any faculty meetings. I don't even talk to Professor Yoon."

I take a deep breath and close my eyes. "I can't jeopardize my future, Wyatt. I don't have a safety net like you do."

When I open my eyes, he's frowning at me, expression turning angry. "That's not fair, Fern. You know about how my family is at risk right now."

I extend my palms his way. "Exactly. I know you're facing a lot and working through a lot of challenges. You have a lot on the line as well. We both need to keep our distance from one another."

Wyatt opens his mouth to say something, but I grab my duffel bag from his back seat. "I'll see you in class tomorrow morning."

———

Except I don't see him in class. I mark him absent and dismiss the group early. Everyone is anxious about midterms, and I set up two study sessions as requested by Professor Yoon. Later that day, I meet with them to review the plan for the rest of the semester. I don't mention Wyatt and my prior relationship with him. Professor Yoon doesn't ask me anything about the recitation.

For two weeks, I spend most of my waking hours in my cubicle outside their office, grading quizzes, not thinking about Wyatt, skipping over his test paper and redistributing it to another TA's stack.

During the final study session before spring break, I'm just about to relax into my role at the front of the room when Wyatt slips into the back. His hat is pulled low, but I can see the dark circles under his eyes like he hasn't been sleeping.

Well, none of us sleep at this point in the semester. I'm sure elite athletes are supposed to be better at it than the rest of us, but I'm feeling the pinch as well, trying to get everything lined up so I can spend next week dealing with my visa and passport applications while my fellow students are all out on a beach somewhere getting wasted.

I briefly wonder if Wyatt will go to a beach for spring

break, if he'll seek distraction or comfort from some bikini-clad girl at a tiki bar. I glance at him and decide that, no, that's not his style. The man who avoids crowds and brings books to a bar will probably spend the week working out and reading some new book about knee injuries in pro athletes.

"All right, folks," I say, dusting off my hands after writing an equation on the chalkboard. We're in a larger room than my typical recitation space, so I have to speak louder to more students. "Who can explain what we do next in this equation?"

A few students in the front row forget that parenthesis come before addition in the order of operations, and I see Wyatt's cheeks flush when I gently correct them. Is he, too, struggling to solve for X? I decide to circle the room, glancing at everyone's paper and pointing out where people need to redo their work. My heart races as I approach Wyatt's desk. I pause in front of his chair. "Can I see?"

He meets my eye, his gaze hot and intense, and moves his hand away. His neat writing reveals that he did the addition and subtraction before multiplying, and I shake my head. "Stay after, and we can talk this through, okay?"

He nods silently, and my breath seems caught in my throat. I take final questions and dismiss the class. A few students linger, checking in with me about the homework problems and the exam review guide. Wyatt remains in his chair at the back of the room, reading a paperback with a soccer ball on the cover, until the last student slips out and closes the door behind them.

We're alone in a lecture hall, both of us silently breathing, looking at one another. Can he feel this tension, too? I realize I miss him, the feel of his hands, the pressure of his lips against mine. "Did you forget Please Excuse My Dear Aunt Sally," I whisper.

He shakes his head. "I never knew it to start with."

I laugh and sit next to him, gesturing for his paper. I write PEMDAS at the top. "Pemdas," I say. "The order of operations. There's a set way you have to approach a problem…"

He looks at me for a long time. I can hear his breath, and I think maybe I can hear his heartbeat, too. "I usually go about things in the wrong order, don't I?"

He stares down at his hand, and I wonder if he's trying not to touch me, trying to restrain himself from placing his palm on my thigh the way I'm struggling not to wrap my arms around his neck. "Well, we're doing things in the right order now, yes? We have to."

Wyatt shakes his head. "I'm not going to be able to do that, Fern." He leans in and before I can blink, his mouth is on mine. His kiss is fierce, the pressure intense, and so, so good. I've missed the smell of him in my nostrils, the feel of his hair sliding around my fingers.

"Wyatt." I breathe his name into his mouth, and he pulls back, his eyes shining and wet as he stares into mine. "We can't."

He nods, and the moment is broken. He draws back, shoves his paper in the pocket of his sweatshirt, and stalks out of the room without another word.

CHAPTER 26
WYATT

I CAN'T BELIEVE I kissed her. I've been withering inside, trying to keep away from Fern for weeks, and then I kissed her. I had to go to the damn study session because I missed class, and she's been very clear that the pass/fail grade for this course is entirely based on attendance. So, then I had to sit and stare at her gorgeous face and brilliant brain as she explained all these concepts to 100 students.

I don't even want one student to look at me, and she stood up there covered adorably in chalk dust while 100 pairs of eyes looked at her.

An unknown number rings my phone as I'm hurrying home from the study session, and I send it to voicemail.

I reach the apartment, stop in the kitchen for a protein bar, and make the mistake of pulling out my phone. I hear Nick's sick voice in the message, telling me he's going to send old videos of him and my mother to the press.

It's all too much: his sneering voice, his threats, the rejection from Fern when she's the one person who has made me feel at ease this entire year. My heart races, and a buzzing sound takes over my awareness. I'm choking on the protein bar, sweating, sinking to the floor in the kitchen, pressing my palms over my ears.

I don't realize I've been shouting until I see Odin's face in front of mine, his hands on my shoulders. I can't hear him, but I see his mouth moving. He's saying my name.

Eventually, he wraps his arms around me. Eventually, I hear his words. "I got you, man. I got you. You're okay, dude."

———

I don't know how much time passes or how I get to the sofa, but once I can hear and see again, my cousins are all pressed against me, concerned. Odin, Stellen, and Gunnar each have a hand on my body, grounding me. Odin, who should be asleep getting ready for the Black and Gold football game this weekend, pulls me in for a hug and plants a kiss on top of my head. "Cuz, you gotta tell us what's going on. This is scaring us, man."

Stellen holds out my phone. "Can you start by telling us what the fuck this is about?"

I blink at him a few times and then sink back into the couch. I close my eyes. Odin says, "Don't make me call Wes to come over here. He says you've been a moody bastard this entire year, and he's not wrong. He's been checking up on you, man. So, let's have it. We stick together, right?"

I nod and pull up the message transcript. I can't handle hearing his voice again. They all read it, cursing. "He's been at this shit all year. He wants money, I think. Or just wants to win? It all started when I tried to change my name." My cousins all sit rapt, silent, waiting for me to continue. They know how much I hate it when the media brings up my past, but they don't know anything about what's currently happening. I tell them how I've been trying to get my name changed, how initially I had to report it in a newspaper, and that's when he really started harassing me. I tell them how I don't want to sign a pro contract with anything linking me to that piece of scum, how I want to be a full and legal part of the Moyer-Stag clan.

"It doesn't matter to me that my dad has me in his will or whatever. It's not about money to me. It's about belonging."

Odin coughs. "Do you think you don't belong with us? Is that what this is?"

I blink at him. "Not entirely. But sort of. I mean, I'm literally the ugly step-child in this situation."

Stellen groans. "Not one of us cares about who your bio dad is, fucker. Do you think we treat Cara like she's not part of the family? She's stuck with us, dude. And you've heard the stories about how all our dads came through for your dad when your mom got the restraining order on Nick all those years ago."

Stellen stands up. "Actually, I'm calling my dad. And yours. This isn't okay, man."

"Please don't, Stell. Odin, come on. I've been handling this on my own."

Odin stands up with Stellen, and Gunnar joins them. Odin glowers at me. "I found you on the floor in the kitchen having a panic attack, Wyatt. You are not okay. That's just facts."

Stellen steps away, and I hear him murmuring into the phone. When I try to get up and stop him, Odin and Gunnar press me back onto the couch. Odin places a hand on top of my head. "I'll sit on you if I have to, but you're going to stay here and endure a Stag family meeting right the hell now."

———

Ten minutes later, my dad and uncles Tim, Ty and Thatcher are crammed in our living room, all gray beards and crossed arms and confusion. Uncle Tim passes out a cardboard box full of fancy bubble water. "This situation seemed to call for San Pellegrino," he says.

My dad frowns at him. "Since when do we drink this shit? I thought you were bringing whiskey."

Uncle Ty shakes his head. "The boys are in season, Hawk. You know they have nutrition plans."

Dad rolls his eyes and pops open his drink, wedging his body onto the sofa by mine. "Want to tell us what this is about, son?"

I shake my head. My cousin Wes appears in the doorway, looking disheveled. Dad frowns at him. "You're in season too. You have a fucking game tomorrow. I'm going to bench your ass."

Wes shrugs. "Some things are more important than soccer." He tells the room how I've been withdrawn since at least August and how I confided in him that I heard from Nick months ago.

Dad curses and crumples his empty can. "Does your mother know about this?"

I shake my head. "No, and this is exactly why I didn't want to get any of you involved. Mom has been through enough." Not only did she have to deal with my abusive father for years, but she also dealt with a sexual harassment crisis in professional soccer. She's been stressed up to her ears, and I even ruined her escape to refresh at the ski chalet. I feel sad and defeated as I tell him, "I'm not going to be the one to upset her. Not again."

Dad looks at me strangely and then, quick as a cat, snatches my phone from my hand. He scowls, and I know he's scrolling through my messages. I worry for a moment that he's reading my conversations with Fern, but then I realize he doesn't give a fuck who I'm sleeping with. He's reading the unknown number messages and transcripts from the calls I never deleted out of fear I'd need them for the police. Because I always knew Nick would come for me. I know he's not safe, and he's not mentally healthy.

A wave of shame crests and splashes over me as my Dad reads the messages and sees my inability to get rid of this guy and the potential to bring down this incredible family who never asked for this kind of drama.

Odin catches my eye as I'm twitching on the couch and moves so he's squatting in front of me, his massive body shielding out the noise in the room as people continue yelling. "Wyatt." Odin squeezes my shoulders. "Do you honestly believe this family won't shred anyone who tries to fuck with one of us?"

I shake my head rapidly. "No, that's not it. I–" A sob catches in my throat, and I just keep shaking my head.

Wes and Gunnar circle around me like we're in a huddle waiting for a medic on the field. Odin rests his forehead against mine. "You're not just a regular cousin. You're my brother, man. And I already have enough fucking brothers."

Gunnar flicks him on the cheek, and Odin barely flinches. Wes rests a hand on my heart, the gesture is warm and surprisingly soothing. Wes says, "Did you honestly think we'd kick you out or something? I'll tattoo my name on your chest right now if that's what it takes, bro. We Stags stick together. No matter what."

Gunnar nods. "No matter what."

The four of them manage to hug me tightly and slowly, the adrenaline works its way out of my system. We start breathing in unison, probably because Odin is loudly conducting a breath symphony with his nose, but the impact is huge.

As my dad shouts for Uncle Tim to read things, I expect to feel another panic attack brewing. But ... I don't. I feel a sense of calm. Like, I'm finally, actually, in good hands. Thatcher walks around picking up empties for recycling. Uncle Ty shoos Odin and Gunnar to bed. They protest but listen to him. Wes agrees to leave when Uncle Tim announces that he's going to handle this immediately.

"What does that mean," Dad asks. "Handle it?"

Uncle Tim scoffs. He's a sports attorney and usually handles contract issues, but I know he has a long history of getting involved when his pro-athlete clients get tangled up with the law. "We will have a restraining order on file by morning," Tim says. "Nicole Kennedy Brady will oversee a media statement in collaboration with your agent." He looks at me. "Where is Brian in all this? Did you at least loop in your agent?" I shake my head. Tim rolls his eyes so hard I'm worried he'll fall over. "We will control this narrative so tightly, Wyatt. What on earth led you to believe you didn't have the full support of the entire Stag family when this first happened?"

Dad places a hand on Uncle Tim's shoulder, calming him before he launches into a Tim-Tirade. "Thank you, brother, for handling the legal and PR details."

Tim's head recoils in shock. "Of course, I'll handle this.

Wyatt, you're my nephew. Nothing is more important than family."

I close my eyes and hear the soft voices of my uncles, and then I hear my apartment door open and close. When I open my eyes, I'm alone in the living room with my dad. And I can't handle the look on his face. "Son," he whispers. I break down in tears.

A sob rips from my throat, the stress of months of these threats and not knowing what to do. Dad is next to me on the couch again, his arm around my shoulders. "Son, your mother and I should have noticed that you were struggling. We should have had your therapists from before on speed dial … or at least kept their cards."

My jaw drops. "Dad, no. You and Mom have been incredible. My whole life, you've been—" A sob catches me off guard as I think about how I loved my dad from the day I met him when I was four. I worshiped him, not just because he was a pro athlete, but because I could tell immediately that he really enjoyed spending time with me. I didn't have words for this stuff as a young kid, but I do now. I see how this family Mom and I found is the real deal, and I'm part of it. For good.

He wraps me in a hug and kisses the top of my head. It's easier for me to talk to him when I'm not looking at his face, so I tell his shirt, "I wanted your name. I wanted it so damn bad. To officially and legally be a full part of this family."

"Wyatt, you've always been my family. You know that."

I nod. "At first, I sort of wanted to surprise you. To sign with a team as Wyatt Moyer, to see my name in ink with a pro team, as the son of the great Hawk Moyer." We both inhale a shaky breath.

He kisses my head again. "You said you made progress on that front?" I nod and explain to him about the student law clinic and how I have a petition for an emergency name change. Dad chuckles, his voice calm and deep, his chest rumbling against mine in this hug. "I'm sure your uncle will get that fast-tracked along with the restraining order."

Dad grins, matching mine. Then his smile fades. "I hate that you know the official terms for these legal situations." We separate but remain next to one another on the couch. Dad lets out a long breath. "I want you to know that you are always more important than anything in my career, son. We're financially secure forever at this point. You know that, right?"

"Ugh. Yeah, Dad. I know."

"Well, then, you have to make me a promise that you won't face anything like this on your own ever again. We move as a herd. Or something like that."

I laugh and stare at the ceiling. "I promise I'll tell you all my troublesome shit from now on."

Dad hums and crosses his arms. I can feel him waiting to say something, practically feel him trying to form the words until he finally asks, "Want to tell me about the woman Birdie and your mother caught you canoodling?" He nudges me with his shoulder. "Or is that a secret, too?"

I cough and wrinkle my nose. "Dad. Come on. Canoodling?"

He shrugs. "Lolly says she's smoking hot."

I drop my head against the back of the couch. "She is. She's really smart, too."

I sit with my father late into the night, telling him about Fern, how I'm not supposed to be with her, how she's moving to England, and I'm hoping to move to

Mexico anyway. He listens, squeezes my thigh, and tells me I'll know the right thing to do when the choice arrives.

"Nothing has to be forever, son. Unless you want it to be." He fiddles with his wedding ring, smiling like a sap freshly in love. It should be gross, but I've always appreciated how into each other my parents are. I wish this message had been the one that sunk in rather than the poison Nick always spewed. I wish I had realized sooner who my real family is.

Dad drapes an arm around my shoulder and rests his head against mine. "Do you know how weird it was finding this family as an adult? I spent my entire life with a father-sized hole in my identity, only to learn I had three brothers."

I smile, trying to imagine what it looked like when Hawk Moyer showed up at a Stag family dinner for the first time. "That must have been a shock to your system."

"Ha! Your Uncle Ty made me go running with them. After a full day of training."

I smile at the thought, even as my thighs ache in sympathy. The four of them still go running together at least once a week, making laps around Highland Park, squabbling. I swallow another lump of nerves and ask, "When did you … accept that you were part of it? Like, really part of it?"

Dad hums and smiles. "They had to force me." He squeezes me. "But I think it was when they all showed up together in court for you and your mom. That was when I realized they were here with me for my dark times as well as my happy sports star moments. You know?"

I don't know how I grew up around all of this unwavering support and love and still managed to cling to the idea that I'm an outsider in their midst. Exhaustion muddles my thinking, and I fall asleep next to my dad on the couch, trusting–for now–that I have his support and that of my entire extended family.

I knew all along that they'd drop everything if I asked them to, but I never wanted to be the cause of any stress for them. But my dad is right—with all of them swinging their collective resources together, there is no need to think any of us will go down for this. I should have realized that they'd *want* to help me, just like I want to help them, whether I'm hauling their asses to Costco or helping Wes chase down the love of his life after a misunderstanding.

When I wake up, the afterglow of support is still with me. I feel hopeful that I can finally move forward with my life on my own terms and that I have the potential for the sort of future I always dreamed of.

Except, the dream of making a name for myself in Guadalajara doesn't feel as bright as it once did. I think instead of Fern's face after I kissed her. She's balancing on a thin wire, and she doesn't have all of this family support that I do. Who and what will pull her back if her involvement with me threatens her goals?

Maybe my dad is wrong about that part of it. I can see the woman I want to be with, and I have no fucking idea how to make that happen without destroying either of our paths.

CHAPTER 27

FERN

I FIND myself downtown with nothing much to do by ten in the morning on the first day of spring break. Turns out, it really doesn't take that long to deal with passport paperwork when you show up with all the forms you obsessively studied online.

I could go back home and binge old seasons of *Call the Midwife* and have myself an ugly cry, or I could hole up in the campus library and get ahead on my work for my remaining classes. There's not much point to getting ahead other than trying to keep my mind off Wyatt and the haunted expression on his face the last time I saw him.

I bury myself in work at the library, finishing papers that aren't due for another month, finalizing calculations on math equations the professors intended to take all semester to solve. Each time a memory of Wyatt's body touching mine bubbles up to my consciousness, I growl, sharpen my pencil, and dig into my scratch paper hard enough to mar the wood surface of the desk.

Eventually, there's nothing left for me to do or grade or

write. And my mind is still a hot mess of anxiety over London and heartbreak over the impossibility of meeting Wyatt when I can't ever have anything meaningful with him. I decide to find Thora, who said she is working concessions for the Forge and Hot Metal pro soccer teams. Of course, it's the pro soccer teams.

I check the time—the games start at 4 p.m. but it's just past noon. Hopefully, I can catch her on the phone, at least before she has to report to work.

"Fern! Where are you?" I hear a lot of noise in the background. She's either on a bus full of drunk people en route to the game, or she's making her way through a tailgate outside the stadium.

I sigh. "The library."

Thora scoffs. "I knew you would be. Hey, someone didn't show up for their shift. Want to come pick it up and at least earn a little money while you're moping?"

Usually, I'd say yes to something like this in a heartbeat, but I'm not feeling up to crowds or feeling able to concentrate on food orders, for that matter. "Thanks, but I'll just go home and mope in peace and quiet."

"Is this still about Mr. Orgasmic?" I hear a slam, and then the background noise fades. Thora has moved somewhere she's able to talk.

"Can you not call him that?" I groan. "But yes. I can't stop thinking about him."

"Look, I get that he's very sad, and that hot possum pout is very attractive. There are many, many examples of this in television canon. But you have shit going on, Fern. What if you find someone else to bang who is actually casual? Just go get your rocks off. Like a man would!"

I rest my head on my hands on the desk in the basically empty library. "I don't think I'm cut out for that sort of sexual freedom, Thor. It's not just that he's sad and it's not just that I want him because I can't have him. I think I like him and his dumb car and the way he looks at me when I talk about math…"

"Ugh, you sound like you haven't heard anything I've told you about the horror stories I see at the legal clinic."

I bite my lip. I know Thora knows a bit about Wyatt's legal challenges. She's right that she's told me all sorts of scary stories about men with legal troubles. Stalking. Tax evasion. Credit fraud. They all manage to find women and dupe them out of their life savings. "The good news here is that I don't have any assets to be duped out of," I tell her.

She sighs. "Trust me. He's not looking to take anything from you. I just mean … I shouldn't say anything." There is another clatter in the background, and I wonder how much longer she'll be able to talk.

"What shouldn't you say? You always say what you shouldn't."

"Ha. Fair." She takes a deep breath. "I just mean … sometimes things escalate. In addition to getting in trouble for boning a student, you might be in danger. Hypothetically. If you hitch your wagon to this guy."

I hadn't considered that if Wyatt might be in danger from his bio father, anyone he cares about would be, too. I have to assume that's what Thora is referring to, based on what Wyatt has told me about how desperately he wants to change his name and be rid of that association as best he can. But how would I be impacted? I groan and start packing up my things. Better to head home and induce a cry via television. "I know you're right that I should just let it all fade into a beautiful memory."

"A beautiful, orgasmic memory you can call up while

you're living the high life in fucking London as a superstar genius fellow in super math school."

She's right. I have a lot on the line, and Wyatt is complicated. Being with him would be complicated and dangerous for many reasons. We hang up when someone starts shouting for Thora to hook up kegs of IC Lite.

I head home, wondering what Thora knows specifically about Wyatt's situation, about what his father might have done to escalate things enough that the student law clinic is aware. My phone starts pinging rapidly when the train exits the tunnel, heading south to my neighborhood.

Mom is checking in, of course, but so is Wyatt.

I stare at the phone, reading his messages over and over again.

> **WYATT**
>
> Are you okay? I wanted to check in.
>
> **WYATT**
>
> Some big stuff happened to me this week. Can I call you?
>
> **WYATT**
>
> You're probably somewhere studying like a good student, aren't you?
>
> **WYATT**
>
> Seriously, though. Can we talk?

I squeeze my legs together, not understanding my reaction to seeing him refer to me as a 'good student.' I nearly miss my stop thinking through all the reasons I shouldn't connect with him outside of class.

But none of those reasons account for the raw vulnerability he showed me telling me secrets about his past.

Things he didn't even tell his family for fear of costing them opportunities. I don't *owe* him a conversation, but I want to have one with him. I want to hear what happened.

We can talk. When's good for you?

CHAPTER 28

FERN

WYATT DRIVES to my neighborhood the next morning to meet me for coffee. It's strange to see him here, where I grew up. My neighborhood is much more focused on football and baseball, as a rule, so he doesn't seem to be at risk for being recognized here as he would on campus with all the rabid college fans.

But when I peek in the window from the sidewalk and see him waiting at one of the tables, he actually looks a lot more relaxed than I've seen him anywhere outside of his family's ski house.

"Hey," I say, pulling up the chair opposite him and sinking into it.

He smiles, wide and bright-eyed, sliding a plate of pastries across the table toward me. "Hey. You hungry?" I shrug, reaching for one, and if possible, his smile widens. "I like that about you, Fern. The way you enjoy your food."

I flush and dab at my mouth with a napkin. "You said some stuff happened? Also, what are you wearing?"

He's got tight-ish black workout pants and a black

jersey I haven't seen before under a plain black zip-up athletic jacket. Usually, he wears university team gear.

He grins. "This is for the soccer combine later today." He bites his lip, expression turning hopeful. "You want to come watch? It's basically a bunch of pro hopefuls in the region doing skills and drills for some scouts from international clubs."

My eyebrows shoot up. "International? Like the Mexican team you were looking at?"

Wyatt nods, pulling off his hat—plain black—and runs a finger through his hair. He doesn't place the hat back on his head, and I hold back the urge to tuck his loose, dark hair away from his forehead. He seems youthful and content. "Did something change for you, Wyatt?" I take another bite of the pastry, and he leans forward, clasping his hands on the table.

"I talked to my dad. And my uncles. About everything." He waves a finger in the air, and I take that to mean his entire situation with his name and the threatening texts and all of it. Wyatt grins. "Uncle Tim pulled a lot of levers. And my Aunt Juniper is a magisterial judge who happened to have night court last weekend." He reaches into his pocket and procures a creased photocopy, which he slides across the table.

"What's this?" I squint to read the fine print, but it's all legalese I'd usually call Thora to interpret.

"My name change. It's official." He pulls the paper back, expression a blend of awe and disbelief. "As soon as I deal with the social security office, DMV, and passport people."

"I just did my passport yesterday! I can help you with the forms." I clap a hand over my mouth, not at all sure why I'd offer that when he's apparently got a whole team of experienced lawyers and lawmakers shepherding him through this process.

But Wyatt reaches for my hand and squeezes it appreciatively. "I'd love that, Fern. Seriously."

I want to bask in the warmth of his skin against mine, but despite his trying to keep a low profile, I can't risk being seen intimately with Wyatt. I tug my hand free and reach for the pastry plate again. "So, you're officially Wyatt Moyer?"

He puffs out a laugh. "Wyatt Stag Moyer. I ditched the middle name for a better one."

"I'm glad for you, truly. Good luck getting your transcripts updated in time for graduation, though." I laugh derisively, and then I realize he probably doesn't care too much about his college transcripts if he's headed off to be a professional soccer player.

"Come to the combine today," he says, his voice low. "I'd love to have you there cheering me on. Yelling Moyer and having it be me you're calling that ..."

I frown. "Won't you have your family there? And your agent and all that?"

He shrugs. "Yeah." He leans forward, closer to me. I can smell his soapy scent, his deodorant and laundry detergent, and his tangy Wyatt aroma. "But they're not you." I take another bite of the pastry, and Wyatt pulls out his phone. "I'm going to text you the info and your name will be at will-call. You don't have to talk to my mom or Grand or Lolly." He winks. "I hope you can make it."

———

Wyatt leaves the coffee shop, and I sit with the tray of buttery deliciousness, worrying about what to do. I'd love to see Wyatt in his element, wearing little shorts. I'm so happy for him that he seems to have dealt with the albatross, although I can't help but wonder if his next steps ought to include some mental health support for the trauma that got him into that state to begin with.

I stare at the details in my phone about the soccer event. It won't be crowded with fans—most likely just family members and press folks. Since I already finished absolutely everything school-related, my only alternative would be another day glued to my couch watching sad television.

I dash home for a hat and sunglasses and make my way to the stadium along the Mon River. By the time I arrive, the athletes have begun their activities. The stands have pockets of families, many holding up signs, but there are a few scattered individuals in the bleachers. I make my way toward the seats behind one of the goals, avoiding eye contact with Wyatt's mother and grandmothers, who I can clearly see up in one of the fancy boxes along with a man who must be Wyatt's father. I can hear them shouting, and I glance to the field in time to see Wyatt receive a complicated pass from a coach.

Wyatt flicks a foot, seemingly effortlessly, and the ball sails into the net right in front of me. I can't help but whoop. And then he cycles through the drill several more times, scoring with each opportunity—sometimes off his left foot, sometimes his right, and sometimes using his forehead to nudge the ball into the net.

He's magnificent out there, totally in control of his body on the field. Other players sometimes crash into him, but he doesn't lose the ball. At times, he moves his foot on top of it, pulling it around the grass like it's attached to his shoe. I see people on the sidelines taking note of Wyatt's work, making phone calls, whispering to one another, and pointing at him. A ball of pride swells in my chest as if I had something to do with his success out there.

One of the coaches blows a whistle and the players break into teams wearing black shirts and white shirts. They start a game, and I wish I had paid attention during any of the times I worked with Thora at these events. I have no idea what's going on with the game, but I can see Wyatt's family pumping their fists and hollering whenever the ball is near him. Wyatt doesn't break his gaze from the field, though. He's focused, determined, dodging around other players with ease.

After a few minutes, he breaks free of a crowd of players, shakes off an elbow, leans back on one foot, and kicks the ball into the corner of the net past the diving hands of the goalkeeper. The stadium erupts into cheers, and I'm caught up in the moment, jumping to my feet to wave my hat around. And then he sees me, and I freeze. The whole stadium seems to melt away as he smiles at me and gives me a little wave. My cheeks heat as he wiggles his fingers in my direction.

Someone calls him off the field, and he disappears into a tunnel. I sit back down and try to pay attention to the action on the field, wondering if I should stay or go now that Wyatt is apparently done with his performance. I've made up my mind to head home and call him later, but someone puts a hand on my arm, stopping me as I go to leave.

It's a man with a camera, which seems to be recording. "Pardon me, miss," he says, his voice indicating a long history with a lot of cigarettes. "You're here with Wyatt De Luca?"

I frown. "I don't know anyone with that name." I try to shove past him, but he chuckles and stands in my way.

"Right, right. Goes by Moyer, doesn't he? I'm doing a little story on his family. Thought it would be good to include some quotes from the girlfriend. What's your name, honey?"

I stare at the man, not knowing how to respond. I know Wyatt is guarded with the press and I can't imagine he'd want to reveal anything about a romantic relationship in the news. He can't really avoid his parents coming up since they're part of the sport. But I feel pretty confident he'd support me telling this guy to fuck off. Except I don't say that because I'm too overwhelmed. I shove past the man and hurry toward the exit gate.

CHAPTER 29
WYATT

I FEEL FUCKING FANTASTIC. I had an incredible morning and Brian pulled me aside the second I stepped off the grass to let me know today is going to be an offer day.

For the first time, the idea doesn't fill me with dread. I've got my mom and dad in the stands, my legal shit sorted out, and a signed document from the courts ordering my biological scum rag to stay the fuck away from me and my entire family.

Plus, my girl is in the stands watching. I know I can't really call her my girl … Fern is my professor–instructor if we're being technical. And I'm moving to Mexico, and she's moving to London. But she's here. She came over to watch me because I asked her to, and that means the world to me.

I'm practically floating when I step outside the locker room to catch my breath and calm down while I wait for Brian to call me up to the conference room to sign paper-work. I lean against the brick of the stadium exterior, smiling at the train going past, and the barges on the river.

This stadium has been my home base for almost my entire life. I spent hours here after school, running around while my parents finished work. Once Dad retired from playing and started coaching, I spent even more time here, running drills alongside the team like some bratty kid. Except, I could always keep up.

I hear a shout and glance toward the sound. I see a woman hurrying toward the light rail station and a crusty man with a camera in hot pursuit.

It's … Fern. What the fuck? "Hey!" I push off the brick and start following them, my cleats loud on the sidewalk. I shouldn't run and risk stumbling in my awkward footwear, but I will if I need to. Fern hears my voice and whips around. Her eyes are wide with concern until she sees me, and I watch as she immediately seems to relax. "Fern, is this guy bothering you?"

"Fern, is it?" The guy pulls out a notepad and starts writing shit down.

"Who the hell are you? Don't say her name."

He smiles and shrugs. "I'm just doing my job, kid."

"Moyer, I've been looking everywhere for you." My agent's voice appears over my shoulder, and I see him approaching from the corner of my eye. He stops beside me, hands on his hips, glowering at the cameraman. "Fuck you, Pella. You trying to get another libel suit? I will sue you before you get to your car."

The man—Pella, apparently—grins and shakes his head. "I just do what I'm told. Take it up with BuzzTalk."

He stalks toward the parking lot, chuckling, and I glare at Brian. "Who is that guy? He was following Fern." I gesture at her.

Brian scowls. "Do I know Fern?"

She opens her mouth, and I place a hand on her shoulder. "She's my fucking friend, and I don't want that guy bothering her. He wrote her name down and took her picture."

Brian nods. "I'll take care of it. This is what you pay me for. I thought we went over that when your dad called me about the name stuff." Brian shakes his head, fingers flying across the screen of his phone. My Uncle Tim appears on the sidewalk with us like he could smell another opportunity to dismantle someone legally. Fern looks like she's going to pass out.

"Hey, can we get her inside? Fern, come on, let me get you some water." I put an arm around her shoulder, but she shakes it off, eyes glittering like she's on the verge of tears. I nod and gesture for her to walk ahead of me and through the door into the stadium offices. We bypass the locker room and head for the elevator, Brian and Uncle Tim whispering about the gossip website, takedown notices, and defamation lawsuits.

They both seem totally casual about this situation, but I can tell that Fern is freaking out that someone is going to write about her and put her photo on the hottest celebrity gossip site around. I walk her toward the conference room, thankful there aren't yet any team reps in here and grab a bottle of water from the bowl on the table. "Tell me what happened," I ask, sitting in one of the chairs and bending to unlace my cleats. I'm done for the day, regardless of what the teams might still be looking for. There's no way I could play right now, all worked up about Fern and the press.

She swallows. "I was cheering for you. He took your picture on the field and then mine and ... asked me things." She takes a big swig of water. "I tried to leave and he followed me. I thought he was going to get right onto the train with me."

I reach for her arm and she yanks it back. I close my eyes, remembering again that while I might have solved all my shit and gotten my ducks in a row, Fern still has everything to lose if people find out she and I are involved. "My family won't let them print anything, Fern. Okay? Do you trust that?"

She rolls her eyes. "The internet is forever, Wyatt. There's probably already a story on TikTok."

"There are always fucking stories about me on TikTok. Why do you think I worked so hard to change my name?"

She stiffens and I lean forward before I remember that she isn't comfortable being touched right now. I hold up my palms. "I'm sorry. I'm just trying to understand what happened."

Brian pokes his head in the door and says abruptly, "Pella filed some gossip piece already, but there's nothing there." He shrugs. "Just says you're the kid of soccer legends Hawk and Lucy, you've got a girlfriend from school, lists her name and the university." Brian squints at his phone. "Okay, it was just updated that ... aw! You guys met in math class?"

Fern turns white.

I stand up and yank Brian's phone from him. "They have to take that down, Brian. There's a situation."

He frowns. "You're supposed to tell me about situations, kid. This is how it works. You tell me about the situations, and I handle them ahead of time."

I drag a hand through my hair. "It's only a situation for Fern."

Her face hardens, and she stands up. "Well, I'm so glad

you see it that way. God, I can't believe I came here." She moves toward the door.

Brian holds up a hand, urging her to stop. "Hey, kiddo, a situation for you is still under my purview. What's going on?"

I open my mouth to tell him that our tryst on New Year's Eve became a huge liability for Fern's future career, but the rest of my family appears in the doorway. Mom, Dad, Odin, Stellen, and even Birdie shove into the room, shouting that the team from Guadalajara is on their way up to the conference room with a contract for me.

Fern shoves through all of them, and I follow her into the hall, feeling ridiculous in my socks and soccer gear while my life is both falling apart and coming together. "Fern, can you just wait?"

She whips around to face me. "For what? The press to publish more about me while you're signing? I have to figure out what I'm going to do, Wyatt. This is serious."

"Brian is going to take care of it. This is going to be fine."

She throws her hands up in the air. "You're so naive if you really believe that they can help me now." She snaps her lips together, closes her eyes, and takes a deep breath. When she opens her eyes, they're cold and distant. "Please don't reach out to me or contact me apart from class. I'm so happy for you and the contract you're about to sign. Thank you for helping me unwind. I hope you can understand why I regret ever trying to do that."

She turns on her heel toward the stairs. I want to follow her, but I'm literally pulled back by sets of arms. My family shouts congratulations that feel hollow and empty as Fern marches away from me.

———

I stare at the pen in my hand that I just used to check off a major life goal. I signed Wyatt Stag Moyer on a professional soccer contract, in black ink, with a boring ass ballpoint pen covered in teeth marks. Who even knows whose mouth was gnawing this Bic.

I should feel … better. I asked my family to give me a minute alone. We're all going out to celebrate later, but I need to calm down. I don't need to look up when I hear a knock on the door–I know it's my dad. I keep staring at the pen as he makes his way to the black leather seat next to me and squeezes my leg. "Hey, kid. Will you sign my jersey?"

I look over to see him holding a Guadalajara jersey. It looks way too big for him. "Where did you get that?"

He laughs. "Brian has a few things in the trunk of his Bugatti."

I sneer at my dad. "Since when does a Bugatti have a trunk?"

Dad ruffles my hair. "Okay, smart ass. The back seat then." Dad pulls a Sharpie from his track pants pocket. "You gonna sign it or what?"

The silky material feels smooth and cool in my hand, a tangible reminder of the dream I just achieved. I don't hold back the grin as I scrawl my name on the back of the jersey, which Dad slips over his Forge polo, a huge smile blooming across his entire face. "I'm really proud of you, you know." And then he sighs. "And I can see that you're upset about the reporter."

I nod and briefly close my eyes, picturing Fern's face. The hurt in her eyes when she left the stadium, the fear of losing everything she's worked for. It tears me apart, knowing that I'm the cause of her pain. "Fern has so much to lose. She … I hate that her knowing me exposes her like that."

Dad nods and taps on the table. He leans forward, his elbows resting on his knees, his eyes searching mine. I can see the worry etched in the lines of his face, but there's also a fierce determination, an unspoken promise there. "I had a similar conflict when I first got with your mother." His mouth tips in a small grin, like the memory is mostly pleasant now. "I don't need to remind you it's important to protect the people you love. Or that you have my full support and any help I can offer to do that."

I swallow a lump and twirl the pen in my hands. "I don't want Fern to suffer because of me, Dad. She's worked so hard for her future, and I can't be the reason she loses everything."

Dad pulls me in for a hug like I'm a kid instead of a grown-ass man who keeps acting like a child. Dad says, "Son, you've got a good heart. We'll figure this out together. Fern's part of the family now, and we take care of our own."

I shake my head against his shoulder. "She asked me to give her space. I want to respect that."

He hums, low and long. "That's a good instinct. But are you sure that's what she's really asking for?"

I nod and sniff through my nose, grounding myself, finally setting down the chewed-up pen. "Yeah. And I think I know how to offer her that distance and still make sure she's okay."

Dad arches a brow and rubs a hand across his stubble. "How's that, son? Want to run your plan past me? Or Uncle Tim?"

I shake my head and stand, clapping him on the shoulder. "I know what I need to do. I'm ready to go find everyone now."

Dad stares down at my feet and I remember that I'm standing around in my socks, and that I came up here right from the field. We both laugh, and he walks me to the locker room to get changed. I know what I need to do, and it's going to piss off my parents, but I know it's the right thing to do–for Fern. For her future. I'll sacrifice whatever I can to make things right for her.

CHAPTER 30

FERN

I DON'T EXPECT anyone to be around during spring break, but after I spent the night crying in my room, obsessively refreshing websites and my email, I can't handle being alone anymore. I travel to the math department, hoping Professor Yoon has decided to work from their office while things are quiet, and the students are away.

They don't seem like the kind of person who goes on a big bender for spring break, and I'm grateful when I see the light shining under their office door. I tap lightly on the wood, knowing I have to face this. Have to come clean about emotional baggage to a mentor who has always been dreadfully matter-of-fact and pragmatic. "Yes?" Their voice sounds muffled and sure enough, I open the door to see them behind a trio of giant monitors. They must be running a complex series of programs.

I step into the room and close the door behind me. "I was hoping I could speak with you." I sink into the chair opposite their desk.

Professor Yoon peeks over the lowest monitor, adjusting their glasses. "Ah, yes. Ms. Montgomery." They stand and walk around to the other side of the desk, leaning against it, hands at their sides, fingers tapping the surface. "I received a strange email yesterday afternoon with a link to an online article that no longer exists."

I nod. I hadn't realized the story had been taken down already. Maybe that means it's okay? That the story lacked veracity?

Professor Yoon seems to be waiting for me to speak next, so I add, "I went to the stadium to support Wyatt. He's one of my students in the recitation."

Professor Yoon nods. "Yes, I took note of that, as well as some official registration updates. Strange. It all showed up in my email at once. You know how I feel about email."

"You hate it?"

They laugh. "I hate most disruptions. This week is for long periods of uninterrupted analysis! Can you just *feel* the data forming patterns?" They clap their hands.

I tuck my hair behind my ears. "I'm not sure how the reporter was able to get information about me...or even if what they wrote was true ..."

Professor Yoon nods. "Yes, there did seem to be a FERPA violation."

"FERPA?" I frown, unfamiliar with that term.

Professor Yoon holds up their hands in a "mea culpa" gesture. "I have been so remiss in your training for this assistantship. The graduate students will have learned that it's a federal offense to release student registration information. But I'm also making a hypothesis that it was not you who told the reporter about Wyatt's enrollment in your class and subsequent withdrawal from school?"

"No, it was definitely not me, but—wait. Withdrawal?"

They frown at me. "Is that not why you're here today? To update your roster? Wyatt *Moyer* and his legal team wrote to update his transcripts with his legal name and then withdrew from the university. Something about professional obligations abroad?" They shrug. "Usually, in these cases, the students simply take an incomplete and finish their degree later. I have no idea why he would totally withdraw from the entire school over a gossip article ... Ms. Montgomery, are you all right?"

I dab at my face, where tears have started to fall down my cheeks. If Wyatt withdrew from school, that means he was trying to keep his word. He made it so he isn't my student, hoping to help me keep my funding. Nobody but my mom has ever made that kind of sacrifice for me. I'm not sure how to handle this. I close my eyes and say, "He did it for me, Professor. Because the truth is that he wasn't just my student. I've been ... involved."

I open my eyes to see Professor Yoon unmoved, blinking, waiting for me to continue. "I met him before the semester began ... and he had that whole name change situation, so I didn't realize it was him on the roster and —"

"And you didn't mention it or switch sections when you had the opportunity?" I shake my head. They tap their fingers on the desk again. "Well, this is a bit of a pickle ... but truthfully, I don't have time to map out all the prongs of this fork." They shrug. "The student has withdrawn and is, in fact, leaving the country. They were in a pass-fail recitation where the grade is based solely on attendance ... I assume you took accurate and unbiased attendance records?" I nod. They nod. "It would be very hard indeed to botch attendance records." They emit a deep sigh and peek over one of the monitors at the program running on the screen. I can see pink lines intersecting with green ones on the monitor as a graph forms, fractal patterns blooming across the three monitors.

"I … don't want special treatment. I broke the rules."

"Did you, though?" Professor Yoon gives their chin another scratch. "The handbook specifies rules for inter-personal relationships between graduate students and undergraduate students, but you are both undergraduates. And like I said, he has left the university. Nobody has filed a complaint. Nobody has reported misconduct."

We are both silent for a few beats. Or maybe a few hours. It all feels agonizingly slow as I sweat in the plastic chair, curling and uncurling my toes inside my shoes while I wait to see what's going to happen with my assistantship. I finally dare to ask, "So, what happens now?"

Professor Yoon takes a deep breath through their nose and holds up their hands again. "Now, you continue your excellent work leading up to the final exam. You seemed to enjoy preparing the students for mid- terms. Would you be interested in leading another large study session the week before finals?"

I blink. "I meant what happens with …" I gesture my hand in a circle.

Professor Yoon glances at their computer again. "Ms. Montgomery, do you think you can figure out how to update the class roster inside the university grading portal? If yes, I would say, please do so and carry on. I'd be most appreciative if you could leave me alone with my prediction model for the rest of the week."

As if that settled the matter, they walk back around to their side of the desk, sitting down with a creak of the chair springs and leaning forward to gawk at the monitors once more. Stunned, and confused, I leave their office and sink into a seat in one of the cubicles. There are no grad-uate students around. No undergrads looking for test grades. Just me and my tattered laptop I pull from my bag. I wait for it to groan into life and log into the grading soft-ware. My screen shows a flashing alert that one of my students has had a status change. In a few clicks, I update Wyatt's name in the system and remove him from my grade roster.

It really happened, then. He's leaving school and moving to Mexico. And I'm carrying on like none of it ever happened.

Except it did happen. I was with him, and it changed me, opening me up to an adoration I never expected and care and comfort I never imagined. And it's all gone again, a reminder that I can either have turmoil and affection or hard work and professional success.

With a sigh, I shut down my computer and make my way to the library. There is still work I can do to prepare for my studies at Imperial College.

CHAPTER 31
WYATT

ALL I DO IS PLAY soccer and use the translate app on my phone. I've been down here for three weeks and already got kicked out of my Spanish class because I kept getting lost and showing up late. I get that I can't be disrupting the other students. I've only got myself to blame.

There's one or two guys on the team who speak enough English to give me shit on the field and joke around a bit, but I miss my cousins. I miss Pittsburgh and being near water. This is the farthest I've ever been from a river for any real length of time. I had no idea how much it impacted my sense of place.

But the soccer is good. Really fucking good. And nothing compares to that feeling of hearing the announcer say my name—Wyatt Moyer—to a sold-out stadium full of rabid fans.

That's what I talk about when my parents call. I send them selfies of myself with kids who asked for my autograph. The first time it happened, I had this vivid memory of meeting my dad for the first time. Mom had gotten tickets to the Forge game, and he had just been signed. I wore that tiny, autographed jersey until I grew enough that the seams started to stretch.

By then, we lived together, and I could have had a thousand jerseys. But that first one felt so special. Someone famous took the time to talk to me. I try to keep that in mind, even if I can't understand half the words these kids say to me.

I'll get used to it.

I'm walking to my rental from the stadium after practice when my phone rings, and I see it's my Grand, so, of course, I pick it up. "I miss you so much," I blurt by way of greeting.

"Hey, guy, I miss you, too. Tell me, what trees you see?" Grand has a thing for hugging trees everywhere she goes, and she goes bonkers for species we don't see a lot in Pittsburgh.

I walk toward a leafy little guy and squint at it. "I don't know what half of these are called," I admit. "This one looks like … floppy?"

"Could it be a corn plant?" Grand sounds so curious, I can almost see her looking up the flora of my new city while we talk.

"I guess? I don't really know Grand."

"Well, you'll send me a picture later, I bet."

I chuckle. "Sure. I'm walking home from practice now."

"I took a guess you would be." I hear a tap turn on. "I had a nice meeting today with the LGBTQ faculty group. Lots of folks there from other departments."

"Oh yeah?" It's unusual for Grand to call me with these sorts of work specifics, even though I was a student at the school where she teaches.

"Mm hm. Professor Yoon was there."

I stop walking. "Is this about Fern?"

She hums. "Sort of. I did mention that they had had you as a student and that you're my grandson. They seemed surprised that you withdrew rather than take an incomplete to wrap up your degree after you get settled."

I adjust my bag to the other shoulder and switch the phone to my other ear. "Grand, I don't really care about the specifics of all that. I'll get it sorted eventually."

"I was wondering the same things as Jae-won, actually. I know we didn't get a chance to talk about school in all the hustle to get you to your new team."

I reach the hotel where I have a long-term rental set up while I'm supposed to be looking for apartments. I take the stairs up to my suite while Grand lists all the reasons a college education is important for everyone, especially when I'm just a few credits shy.

"Look," I tell her, clicking the door shut and flipping the deadbolt. "It was the easiest way for me to get on the road quickly," I lie. The truth is withdrawing from school was worlds easier for Fern. If I made it so I was no longer her student, there was no chance for repercussions from the BuzzTalk article.

Although, Brian tells me the writer and editor are getting slammed *and* someone from the university is in trouble for releasing information about me. Who knew I had federal rights to privacy about my enrollment?

"Well," Grand continues, "Jae-won and I also have a student in common. Fern."

"I forgot you had Fern in class this semester." I sink onto the edge of the bed, trying not to put my grandmother on speaker so I can look at photos of Fern on my phone.

"Yeah. She's doing some really cool interdisciplinary work with advanced pattern modeling and art forgery identification. I'm writing her a letter of introduction for someone at her graduate program in London."

My heart swells at that, the idea of Fern getting a leg up. I like that it's based on something she did with her own incredible brain and work ethic. Nothing to do with me pulling strings or swinging my family name around. Fern probably likes that, too. "I'm sure she's going to be a rockstar over there," I mutter.

Grand hums again. "Well, I'll let you go. I'm supposed to remind you that the Stag herd is flying down for your match against Cruz Azul, and your Uncle Tim wants to have a board game night afterward."

I scoff. "Sure. Let's sling colored tiles around while the fam is on vacation."

Grand laughs. "Azul is a fun game. But I think you're right that the beach would be a better choice."

"Are you and Lolly coming down with them?" I can't figure out if I hope she is or isn't … I want to grill her for more information about Fern but also avoid all discussion of her until she's settled into her fellowship and safely funded where she needs to be.

"Nah. Gotta get ready for finals. Love you, Wyatt."

"Love you, too."

———

The next few days are a blur of training, film, and trying to understand what Coach is asking of me. The team here has a very specific style of play, really aggressive offensively, and I'm up to the challenge. I just … am slow to process the strategy through the language barrier.

So, I'm mentally exhausted when I walk back to the hotel the night before the match and totally unprepared to find my family sprawled out in my suite.

"The hell?" I barely get the curse out before I'm bombarded by hugs and hair ruffles. Even my sister wedges herself in for a hug. "Shouldn't you be in Palo Alto? I thought you have camp?"

Birdie shakes her head. "You got your weeks messed up, dude. I had this next week off to be home for your senior night stuff …" She shrugs, and Mom gives her a side hug.

"We're all excited to spend time with you here and see you play, babe." Mom stretches up to kiss my cheek, and I bend over to let her.

My cousin Wes and his girlfriend, Cara, are sprawled on my sofa, watching a British Premier League match on the television on mute. "We've both got a bye week," he says without looking away from the screen.

I grin, happy to see my space full of family, even if it's a little shady that someone from the staff let them in here. I guess my parents have sway with fans of La Liga. Dad pushes off the wall, waiting until everyone peels off me to give me one of his crushing hugs, lifting me in the air with a grunt. "Wow. I keep forgetting you're big now."

I grin, wrapping my arms around his waist and lifting him easily. We both laugh as I set him down, and he says, "All right, all right. Show off."

I show them the view from my window—boring apart from the trees Grand cooed over. I show them my gear, feeling a swell of pride just seeing the name MOYER in glossy white vinyl on the back of my practice jersey. My game kit will be hanging in my locker when I get to the stadium, and I like that they'll see that, too.

But Mom looks wistful, and Wes barely glances away from the game. Which, to be fair, is tied with just a few minutes of injury time remaining. Birdie tells me she ordered room service since she and my cousins are on a meal plan. I am supposed to be, too, but I've been slipping a little now that I have access to incredible street tacos.

We cram around the table, and my family is oddly quiet and polite. "You guys are acting weird," I tell them around a mouth full of corn.

Dad and Mom exchange a glance and she sighs, reaching for my hand. "We talked to Grand, you know. We hadn't realized you withdrew from school."

I point at Wes, who never even finished his senior year. "We already went through all this with him last year. My body only has so many years to do this kind of work. Dad, you didn't finish school, either!"

He nods. "You're right. But I also never dropped out to protect someone from a publicity scandal incited by a criminal in violation of his no-contact order."

"Wait, what? Nick was behind this?" I throw my napkin across the table, feeling nauseated at the thought of that man somehow determining my life path in any way.

Mom closes her eyes and takes a deep breath. "He tipped off the reporter. He was able to speak with the admissions office, too, since he had your personal information." She points a finger at the ceiling. "But your Aunt Juniper and your dad's foundation are mandating training for any public-facing university employees, reminding them about the rules and who is allowed to access student data."

I rock back on my chair, tugging on my hair. I thought I was past all this mess. The stress of it creeps up and over me, not quite to the level where I had that panic attack back in Pittsburgh...but not far from it.

Dad squeezes my arm. "I want to say a few things, okay? First of all, you know I started my career in the UK. The competition is excellent, the coaching is world-class, and there's no language barrier for you."

I bristle at his mention of the UK. I stare at him and Mom, wondering how much they know about Fern and if it's weird to feel excited about this suggestion.

Dad folds his hands on the table and continues. "The shared language would be really useful when you're working on your mental game." He points to his head. "Your mother and I feel sick that we didn't check in with you about your past, what you've been through."

I growl. "I'm over all that. You did your part. I had therapy for years." I'm not really over it ... I'm just distracted by thoughts of moving closer to Fern without any risks to her career. But she hasn't reached out, and she told me she wanted space. She might not appreciate me showing up in town with my caravan of issues.

Wes snorts. "Dude, I'm in therapy now. I don't know how anyone would deal with the pressure of pro-sports without therapy, and that's without someone trying to sabotage my life."

Cara smiles sadly and nods. "Also, in therapy. And, you know, someone did try to sabotage my life. So, I'm here if you ever want to talk about that."

"I definitely don't want to talk about it. I came here to forget about all of that. Look, I appreciate that you're all concerned about school, and I definitely appreciate that you're behind me with legal resources. I can't wait to play tomorrow with you here. Family is everything to me. You all know that."

Dad crosses his arms, and Mom leans her head on his shoulder. "You can't run away from those challenges, Wyatt. They're faster than you, and they have more endurance. The only way to slay those dragons is to sit down with them and talk through it. With professional support."

"Thanks for the pep talk, Coach." I leave the table and head into my bedroom, slamming the door.

———

Eventually, I hear my family head out of my room, leaving me alone with the clawing, sickening realization that they're right. About all of it. I fucking know I need to get my head straight about all this stuff with Nick, and I have no idea why I'm reeling at the thought of starting up therapy again.

That's a lie. I know it's hard work and exhausting, and they're right that I'm using all my extensive energy on my game and navigating a new space where I can't even read the menus at restaurants. If I'm honest, I'm not trying too hard to assimilate here. At least half of my sour mood stems from missing the competent, kind, and sexy-as-hell math genius whose life I almost blew up. I pull out my phone and stare at a picture I snapped of us at the ski house. My heart lurches in my chest, missing her. Is it even possible for me to transfer to the same city as Fern without pissing her off?

I search her name online and smile, reading the profile her university put up about her interests in … advanced math words I don't know how to pronounce. London is a big place, and I'll be traveling fifty percent of the time. If she tells me to fuck off, I can disappear from her life just as easily there as I can here. But what if she's happy to see me? What if things could be better once both of us have a stronger foundation?

I wait a few hours to see if any of this starts to feel ridiculous, but the opposite happens. I start to get excited about the potential of a transfer. Of a change in plans that might bring me near the best woman I've ever met.

I text Brian to see if there's space in my contract to put me on loan.

CHAPTER 32
FERN

I CAN'T BELIEVE I let Thora talk me into working concessions at the Black and Gold game. The stadium is packed with rowdy students and alumni, all here to cheer on our football team one last time before graduation. The air is electric with school spirit, but I'm just not feeling it.

"Come on, Fern,". Thora nudges me as we fill up cups with ice. "This is our last hurrah! We've got to make the most of it."

I force a smile, but my heart's not in it. "What does it say about us that our hurrah is working while other students party?"

She laughs. "Totally on brand for us."

I should be over the moon right now - I've secured my fellowship in London, I'm on track to ace all my classes, and I'm about to graduate with honors. But all I can think about is Wyatt.

Thora must sense my mood because she gives me a knowing look. "You're thinking about him again, aren't you?"

I bite my lip, feeling the heat rise in my cheeks. "I can't

help it, Thor. What we had ... it was intense. I've never felt that way before." This is the first I've felt up to discussing it out loud. I've spent the weeks since spring break in a sort of waking coma despite Thora's efforts to drag me out of my own funk.

She sighs, handing a customer their change. "I get it, babe. But you said it yourself - it's for the best. You're both heading in different directions."

"I know, I know. It's just ... he gave up so much for me. He left school, Thora. To protect me." My throat tightens at the memory. I don't know what to make of his gesture and subsequent disappearance. I did tell him not to contact me. I squirm, wondering if I should reach out to him.

Thora's eyes soften. "That just shows how much he cares about you, Fern. But you can't let that hold you back. You've worked too damn hard to get where you are."

She's right; I know she is. But that doesn't stop my mind from wandering to stolen moments with Wyatt - the way his hands felt on my skin, the intensity in his eyes when he looked at me, the depth of the connection between us. Was that love? Do I love him? I don't even know how to recognize that emotion.

Thora must read my thoughts because she bumps my hip with hers. "Hey, no more moping. There will be plenty of hot, smart, non-student men in England. Trust me."

I can't help but laugh. "Speaking of England, did you sort out your paperwork for the Rhodes fellowship?" Thora was accepted into the program because she's a badass but hit some hiccups with her visa and passport.

Her face splits into a huge grin. "Nothing will keep me from Oxford, baby!" She takes a breath. "But I'm still working on the identity verification. Turns out when your parents are drunk when you're born, they spell shit wrong on the paperwork."

"Thora!" I throw my arms around her. "That's a nightmare. I hate that for you."

We ignore the line of customers for a moment. She grips my hands. "I'm on it. I'm not above asking everyone I know for help. We're going to tear up London together," she vows, eyes sparkling. "Different schools, not too far apart. We've got this."

I feel a rush of affection for my best friend. She's been my rock through all the drama with Wyatt, never judging, always supporting. Knowing she'll be with me in London makes the whole thing seem less daunting. "Please let me know if I can help."

"Well, well, well. If it isn't our favorite bartenders." A familiar voice breaks through our conversation. I look up to see Wyatt's cousins grinning at us from the other side of the counter. I pinch my lips together and wave nervously.

"What can we get for you boys?" Thora asks all business. I don't think she recognizes them.

As they place their order, I can't help but study their faces, looking for traces of Wyatt. The family resemblance is strong, but none of them have his particular brand of intensity. Which makes sense, since he's not biologically related. But they all definitely have a similar swagger.

"Are you here to see Odin play?" I ask, trying to keep my tone casual. Thora turns at that, brow furrowed.

Stellen nods. "Yeah, it's his last home game. He's hoping to make a big impression before the draft."

Thora groans audibly. "Odin fucking Stag. I should have put it together." She smacks her forehead. Stellen, Gunnar, and I stare at her. "He's in my arguments class.

He's the one driving me crazy, refusing to do anything on the final project."

I glance at her. "I thought you *wanted* to take over and do everything?"

She waves a hand. "I'm going to handle it. What do you other Stag assholes want to eat?"

They laugh and order a bunch of food, which I start to prepare as Thora takes their money.

Just then, a collective gasp rises from the crowd. I whip around to the TV screen just in time to see Odin crumple to the field, clutching his leg. The announcer's voice blares over the speakers. "Odin Stag is down. It looks like a serious injury, folks."

The Stags go pale, abandoning their food and rushing off to find their family. I turn to Thora, expecting to see relief that she won't have to deal with their antics anymore. But her face is stricken.

"Oh god, Fern. What if I cursed him? What if this is my fault for complaining about him?" Her voice shakes.

I pull her into a tight hug. "Hey, no. This is not on you. Injuries happen in sports all the time. It's a risk they all take."

She nods against my shoulder, but I can tell she's not convinced. The weight of the moment hits me - in the blink of an eye, everything can change. All those dreams, all that potential, can disappear in an instant. My heart aches for Odin and his family. But I can also see how the weight of Thora's and my own dreams has impacted us. We both have a hair trigger when it comes to catastrophe. What's that line from *Dirty Dancing* about balancing on shit?

Odin will come out of this just fine, but Thora and I don't really have people to pull us out if we start sinking.

"Come on," I tell her. "Let's focus on this shift, and then we'll take a look at your paperwork drama."

We both finish our shift robotically, and I don't even think twice about splurging for a ride share home rather than fighting the crowds on the train from the stadium. Mom is waiting for me with grilled cheese sandwiches, but her face falls when she sees me walking in the door.

I sink onto the couch with a groan and Mom walks over, handing me a plate. She perches next to me on the couch, waiting for me to spill my guts.

The scent of melted cheese and buttered bread wafts toward me, and my stomach grumbles in response. I take a bite, savoring the perfect blend of crispy, golden-brown bread and gooey, comforting cheese. I swallow, then tell her someone I know got hurt in the game today. Mom frowns. "That's awful, dear. But you seem more upset than I'd expect for … something like that."

I take another bite. She always gets the bread toasted perfectly. Crispy and brown, crackling with flavor. I swallow again. "It's Wyatt."

Mom raises her brow. "The person who took you on your getaway?" She nudges me with her shoulder, and I nod.

"He's not just *a* person, though, Mom. I think he's *my* person. And he left." I don't add *because I told him to leave.* She tilts her head to the side, listening. I set the plate down on my lap. "He left school, and I think he left the whole country. He was trying to get a job in Mexico … I haven't looked." I blow a raspberry with my lips. "I know it's crazy, but I miss him, and I can't imagine my life without him now."

Mom puts an arm around my shoulders. "I didn't

realize you felt so intensely about someone. Why didn't you tell me?"

I shrug. As I sit on the couch, the weight of Wyatt's absence settles heavily on my chest. It's like a piece of me is missing, and I can't shake the feeling that I've lost something precious. "It's all very new. Or … it was. It's all over now. And I guess I'm sad about it."

Mom's brow furrows with worry as she listens to me, her hand gently rubbing my back in soothing circles. I can see the love and concern in her eyes, and it's a comfort to know that she's always here for me, no matter what. She's my constant. But I still ache. Mom rests her head on my shoulder. "Oh, honey. Love is never easy, is it?" I shake my head, and she squeezes a bit tighter. "I think you just need to give it time. If you two are meant to be, you'll find a way to make it work."

As I lean into my mother's embrace, her words echo in my mind. Maybe she's right. Maybe Wyatt and I just need time to figure things out. But the pinch in my heart reminds me that waiting is easier said than done and that I'm not in a position to go where he is. Not for the next five years.

The next morning, I wake up feeling a bit more settled, but the weight of Wyatt's absence still lingers. I know I need to keep moving forward, so I text Thora and suggest we visit the Stags to check on Odin.

At least it will give me something to focus on besides my own heartache. Thora and I head for the Stags' apartment, a tin of cookies in hand. "I just want to check on him," Thora says, shifting nervously. "And apologize for any bad juju I might have sent his way."

I rub her back soothingly. "It's going to be okay, Thor. He'll appreciate the gesture."

"I'm still not doing his portion of the project," she mutters.

I nod, knocking on the door. "That's fine, babe." I knock again.

When the door swings open, it's not Stellen or Gunnar standing there. It's Wyatt.

I feel the air leave my lungs in a rush. He looks just as shocked to see me, his eyes widening. But then a slow, warm smile spreads across his face, and my knees go weak.

"Fern. Hi." His voice is soft, almost reverent.

"Hi," I manage, my heart pounding.

Thora groans beside me. "You two are so obvious." She grabs the cookies from my hand. "Is Odin here? We brought snacks."

Stellen appears behind Wyatt. "Snacks?"

Thora peers past him. "Yeah. For *Odin*. Is he here?"

Stellen winces and looks at Wyatt, who starts scratching at the back of his neck. Wyatt says, "He tore his Achilles."

I frown. "That doesn't sound good."

Stellen shudders. "He had surgery last night. Gonna be months of rehab. He's still in the hospital for observation. Are those cookies?"

Thora clutches them tighter, and my stomach twists at the thought of Odin's injury. He's always so playful, but I know he must be serious about his sport to play at this level.

"I'm heading to the hospital to see him," Stellen says. "Want to come?"

Thora nods, casting me a significant look as she follows him out the door, Gunnar trailing behind. And then it's just me and Wyatt, alone in the apartment.

"I missed you," he says without preamble. "So much. But I was trying to respect your boundaries, give you space ..."

"I missed you, too," I admit, my voice catching. "I can't stop thinking about you, about us."

His eyes search mine, full of longing and hope. "Come sit?"

I nod, letting him lead me to the couch. The apartment is a mess, with half-packed boxes scattered everywhere. "Is someone moving out?"

He sighs, running a hand through his hair. "Yeah. I didn't take much with me to Mexico, so I need to get the rest of my stuff." He looks at me. "Did you know I went to Mexico?"

I shake my head, then I nod. My mouth is dry, and when I try to talk, no words come out.

Wyatt gestures around the room. "I signed with Guadalajara after the combine. The same day as all that press drama. Hey, Fern, I'm so sorry for any stress I caused you. You shouldn't have to feel unsafe just knowing me, coming to a sporting event."

My heart races. I can feel the pulse of it thumping in my ears, which are hot and sweaty all of a sudden. "I ..." What am I going to tell him? That I didn't feel unsafe? That's not true. But I felt more unsettled when he disappeared, even though I flipping told him to leave me alone.

Wyatt fills the silence. "I, um, have some shit to sort out."

He taps his head. "I'm a little fucked up from what happened with my ... with Nick." My face softens at his admission, and I reach for his hand, squeezing it, relishing the feel of him.

Wyatt swallows. "I actually have a trade in motion. I was going to have my stuff sent to me from the apartment ... but I flew home last night when I heard about Odin." He trails off, the weight of his cousin's shattered dreams hanging in the air.

"I'm so sorry," I whisper, squeezing his hand again.

He grips my fingers, drawing strength. "It's the risk we all take, you know? Every moment on that field is a gift. We never know when it might be our last."

His words hit me like a punch to the gut. Life is so fragile, so precious. And I know that so why don't I ever translate that to things that bring me joy? Why are we wasting time apart when we could be together?

As if reading my mind, Wyatt takes a deep breath. "Fern, I need to tell you something. I'm transferring to West Ham United. For at least a year."

"In London? But I thought ..." My head spins, trying to process this new information.

"The language barrier was too much in Mexico on top of everything else I'm dealing with, and West Ham has an amazing psychology team I'll be able to work with." He smiles and turns so he's facing me directly. "But also, I want to be close to you," he says, his eyes boring into mine. "While you chase your dreams, I want to be there to support you in whatever way you'll let me. Because I lo-"

I cut him off with a fierce kiss, pouring all my pent-up emotion into it. He responds instantly, his arms coming around me, holding me tight. In that moment, everything falls into place. This is where I'm meant to be. He's not a roadblock. This relationship feels necessary, a vital part of me moving forward.

None of the challenges that happened this year have been his fault or my fault alone. We made these choices together, and every step of the way, we've overcome obstacles. This reality sinks in as I press my lips to his, clinging to his shirt, and moaning into his mouth. With Wyatt by my side, I feel like I can conquer anything.

When we finally break apart, I'm breathless and giddy. "I love you, too," I whisper against his lips. "I think I always have."

His answering smile is blinding. Wyatt is my home, my heart, my forever. As he lowers me back onto the couch, our bodies tangling together, I know that whatever the future holds, we'll face it together.

CHAPTER 33
WYATT

AS I LOWER FERN ONTO the couch, our bodies intertwined, I can hardly believe this is real. After all the heartache and uncertainty, she's here in my arms, telling me she loves me. I've been so consumed by my own nightmare that I never stopped to believe or even hope I could have something like this.

My hands roam her body, reacquainting myself with every curve and contour. Her skin is just as soft as I remember, her scent just as intoxicating. I trail kisses down her neck, savoring the little gasps and moans that escape her lips.

"Wyatt," she breathes, her fingers tangling in my hair. "I need you."

Those three words set me on fire. "Yeah, you do, gorgeous." I sit up just long enough to tug my shirt over my head before diving back in, capturing her lips in a searing kiss. Her hands explore my chest and my abs, leaving trails of heat in their wake.

I remember how she has trusted me for this kind of intimacy, how I'm the one who made her feel safe enough to let her guard down when all she's ever done is build a fortress to protect her on a path to a different sort of life. I slow down, savoring the feel of her, physically and emotionally.

We undress each other slowly, reverently, as if we're unwrapping the most precious gifts. When we're finally skin to skin, I have to take a moment just to look at her, to memorize every detail of this perfect woman beneath me.

My eyes drink in the sight of her luscious curves, the soft swell of her breasts, the dip of her waist, the tantalizing flare of her hips. I run my hands along her sides, marveling at how her body yields to my touch, supple and pliant, but I know she has a core of steel inside.

This gorgeous body covers an unshakable strength and resilience. Fern has become my favorite story, one I want to read over and over again, even as it's still being written. She's faced so many challenges and overcome so much, and she's never lost her warmth, compassion, and incredible capacity for love. Or is that just for me?

As I lower my mouth to her breast, taking a nipple between my lips, she arches beneath me, a breathless moan falling from her lips. Her nipples harden so fast. I pinch them, loving the way they respond to my touch. Her eagerness lights me on fire and sets off a primal need to pleasure her, to worship every inch of her. Fern has become as vital to me as my family, familiar and comforting ... but meeting very, very different needs.

I swing my attention on her breasts, licking, suckling, teasing, until she's writhing beneath me, her nails digging into my shoulders. The contrast of her soft flesh against my hard muscles is intoxicating, a heady reminder of how perfectly we fit together in every way.

"You're so beautiful," I whisper, trailing kisses down

her stomach, memorizing the way her muscles quiver under my touch. "I love you so much, Fern."

Her eyes, dark with desire, shine with unshed tears. "I love you, too. More than anything."

I pour all my emotion into the next kiss, letting my actions speak louder than words ever could. As I settle between her thighs, the heat of her drawing me in, I'm once again struck by the incredible gift of her love, her trust, her surrender.

"I'm on the pill," she whispers, breath hot on my ear. "And there's never been anyone but you …"

I draw back. "What are you saying?"

She shrugs. "I want to feel you inside me with nothing between us, Wyatt. Nothing but us."

I swallow, trying not to explode. "I get checked all the time. I'm healthy, Fern. And there hasn't been anyone since you." I blink away moisture and smile at her. "You're it for me, baby."

She smiles and licks her lips, reaching for me. I hiss when she wraps a palm around my length and moan as she guides me between her thighs. I lock eyes with her and sink inside, the sensation so overwhelming I collapse on top of her, giving her my full weight.

"I like how heavy you feel on top of me," she says, wrapping her legs around me. I kiss her throat and settle onto my forearms so I can see her, wanting to see her face while we do this.

We move together like a symphony, our bodies perfectly in sync. Each touch, each caress, each thrust is a declaration of love, a promise of forever. The way she embraces me, her soft curves molding to my hardness…it feels like an unbreakable connection.

When we finally come apart in each other's arms, spent

and sated, I hold her close, marveling at the way she fits so perfectly against me. Her body, so soft and yielding, is like a safe haven in a world that's been so harsh and merciless.

This is where I belong. She is home.

———

I pace the arrivals gate at Heathrow, my heart racing with anticipation. I tried bringing a book, but there's no way I can concentrate on reading it, so I shove it in my back pocket and stare at the arrivals board again. Fern's plane landed twenty minutes ago, and I know it's only a matter of time before she clears customs and makes her way to me.

The past month has been a whirlwind. Between settling into my new team, finding a flat, and starting sessions with the psychologist, I've barely had a moment to catch my breath. I've literally been counting down the days until Fern gets here. She sent me 30 images from the art class she took with Grand and told me to put one up on the wall every day until we could be together. Sort of sappy, but I like having someone to be that way with.

I call her every day, even if the time zones are hard with my training schedule. Fern doesn't seem to sleep anymore, so it worked out. She's been wrapping up her finals and packing up her life in Pittsburgh while I've been scoping out all the places I want to show her in London. I offered to fly her mom out here with her, but Ms. Montgomery doesn't have a passport yet. She and Fern are making plans and soaking in their time together, and I hope they'll let me help out when they're ready. What else am I going to do with this sort of paycheck?

Finally, I see her emerge from the sliding doors, her

face lighting up when our eyes meet. I rush forward, sweeping her into my arms and spinning her around, for once not caring about people staring. "You're here," I murmur against her hair, breathing in the scent of her. "You're really here."

I'm vaguely aware of a few people snapping photos of us. One of the first things I talked about in therapy was my aversion to the press, and how important it is for me to make a good impression with fans. I have all sorts of mental exercises I work through to remind myself that it's okay for the world to see me successful and happy and that my father can't take that from me.

So now, I let it happen. Thankfully, nobody tries to interrupt us. Until my phone emits a quacking sound. "What the hell?" I glance down to see a group text from my cousins.

YOUNG STAG GROUP CHAT
ODIN

Did you know I can manipulate your notifications from afar? You're still on the family plan!

STELLEN

Epic.

GUNNAR

We're going to video call you during family dinner this weekend. Tell Fern she has to tune in.

ODIN

Can you put her on the family plan so I can fuck with her phone notifications, too?

Reading over the exchange, Fern laughs, a joyful sound

that sends my blood buzzing. "I'm here. And I'm not going anywhere."

I cup her face in my hands. "Welcome to London, love. Ready for the adventure of a lifetime?"

Her smile is brighter than the sun. "With you? Always."

Hand in hand, we make our way out of the airport, ready to take on the world together. It's not going to be easy. She's in an intense academic program. She's gonna be a hot doctor. And my life is intense. But I know we can handle anything as long as we have each other.

Fern is my rock, my guiding light, my forever home. And as we step out into the bustling streets of London, I feel a sense of peace wash over me. This is exactly where we're meant to be, side by side, chasing our dreams and building a life together.

She and I are forging a new legacy, one that's entirely our own—one that recognizes the power of love, resilience, and the unbreakable bonds we share. It's a legacy I'm proud to call mine...ours.

EPILOGUE: WYATT

5 MONTHS LATER

"I CAN'T BELIEVE you splurged for first class." Fern curls to face me on the comfortable bed in the plane. We've shifted things around a bit to be next to one another and the little pod is surprisingly cozy and private.

I tuck back a strand of hair that has sprung loose from the sleep mask she hasn't yet pulled over her eyes. "What's the point of earning all this pro soccer money if I can't take care of you?" She rolls her eyes and tugs the mask over her face, wriggling a bit under the downy blanket. Her body slowly starts to relax against mine, and I kiss the top of her head before tugging my own mask in place.

I only get a few days off between matches this Christmas, so if I'm going to visit my family with Fern, I want to be as comfortable as possible. Flying first class from London to Pittsburgh is the first big splurge I've made, and I don't think I can ever go back now that I've had the incredible food and lay-flat seats .

I don't sleep much on the flight, but I enjoy the long stretch of time with Fern in my arms. She technically lives in the student housing on her campus but spends what nights she can at my flat between my travel commitments. This cuddle fest above the Atlantic is a real luxury.

When we land in Pittsburgh, I try to play it cool, so I don't tip Fern off to the next round of surprises. We get to exit the plane first, which means we sail through customs to find my cousin Wes waiting to give us a ride, along with …

"Oh my god! Mom!" Fern runs to hug her mother, dropping bags on the floor. Wes grins and hugs me around my own bags before stooping to pick up Fern's. She and her mom are dancing around, crying, and squeezing each other. I try to gently usher them to the side, so we don't block people coming through the security doors.

"I missed you so much," Fern and Heather Montgomery sob in unison. Grand and Lolly finally helped Fern's mom get her passport, so she's going to fly back with Fern in January to tour around London a bit before the spring semester, or Hilary Term, as Fern tells me they call it. I'm sending them both first class, obviously.

The final surprise for Fern is our destination. Rather than exit the highway for Pittsburgh, Wes keeps heading east toward our ski house. Fern and her mom are so busy talking in the back seat that they don't notice until we hit the snowy side roads in the mountains. Fern presses her face to the window and coos. "Wyatt Stag Moyer, I thought we were staying with your parents?"

I grin at her from the front seat. "We are. We're staying with my parents in their ski house. Along with Wes's parents, Odin's parents, Petey's parents … Grand and Lolly …"

"Okay, okay. Wow." Fern clasps her mom's hand. "Are you ready for 21 people in a huge house? Because I don't know if I am."

Heather laughs. "I went to a Sunday dinner with all of them last week to help plan Christmas." She pats Fern's hand. "It'll be fun."

Wes navigates his Jeep carefully up the icy roads, and it doesn't take long before we see light glowing from the massive windows of the Stag Chalet. Fern and Heather both sigh. I can already feel the familiar, comfortable warmth. And then Wes opens the front door, and chaos slams into us. But I smile because that's familiar, too.

Aunt Alice shoves a drink into Heather's hand and ushers her off to sit by the fire with Aunt Emma and Lolly. Stellen and Gunnar grab all our bags and complain about having to stay in the bunk room while Fern and I get our own space in a new room we all agreed would be better served as a sleeping space than a room just for foosball.

I'm about to feel compassion for Gunnar, but he slings me over his shoulder and drops me in the hot tub, fully dressed as the rest of my family watches and laughs. I spit a mouthful of hot water in his face, grinning, and he strips to his boxers and climbs in with me. It's good to be home, with family.

The past few months have been simultaneously incredible and incredibly difficult. I've got a lot of mental stuff to work through, but I'm learning that therapy is a lot like any other sort of training. I put it on the schedule, I show up, I do the work, and I feel the results. I've been playing the best soccer of my life with West Ham, and they just bought out my contract for four years, which means Fern and I don't have to search for our next home base together until she's done with her PhD.

She emerges from the house with a huge smile on her face and fluffy towels draped over one arm. "Are you okay in there?"

"I'd be better if you were in here with me instead of this guy." I hook a thumb at my cousin, who tries to dunk me, gives up, and sprawls against the back edge of the tub.

Fern shivers a bit and looks at Gunnar. "No Odin this year?"

He shakes his head. "Not this time."

Fern opens her mouth to add something, but a door opens above us, and my mom pokes her head out into the dark. "Dinner is in five minutes. Whoever is out here, come in and wash your hands."

Fern laughs. "I love that washing hands is the important to-do item before dinner when you're fully clothed in the hot tub."

I hop out of the water and accept one of the towels from my ladylove. I consider taking them both and leaving Gunny to freeze, but I opt for kindness. By the time I'm changed into dry sweats and have clean hands, the entire family is seated at the huge wooden table.

Wes has his arm around Cara, Birdie steals sips from Dad's wine ... even Uncle Tim seems relaxed with his whole family under one roof. A crackling fire and a massive pine tree decorated in silver-glitter popsicle sticks from our youth give the entire room a cozy vibe. Fern squeezes my leg, and I'm glad to see she doesn't look nervous at all. She and her mom are used to quiet holidays with just a few people, but everyone here has accepted them as part of the growing family.

I've got enough therapy under my belt to see it was always this way. I've always been welcome here, part of the fabric.

Uncle Ty approaches the table with a huge platter of meat, Aunt Alice right behind him with a massive pot of ... something I'm sure I'm allowed to eat because she's amazing that way. Uncle Ty holds up the knife like a microphone and says, "Before we dig in, someone needs to hand me their phone so we can send a picture to Odin."

Alice sets her food on the table and reaches into her back pocket. "I've got you covered. But you've got longer arms."

He grins, turns, and extends the phone as far out as he can, squints at the screen, and then leans back to make more room. "I think we can get everyone in. Heather, Fern, squeeze in a bit more. More than that. Perfect."

He snaps a few shots, and I know half of us will have crossed eyes or pursed lips, but the result will be perfect: flawed and overflowing, with plenty of room for everyone.

Thank you for reading Forging Legacy! Up next is Odin and Thora in Forging Chaos. (Turn the page for a sneak peek!)

Can't get enough of Wyatt and Fern? My newsletter subscribers get a bonus scene! Visit LaineyDavis.com to sign up or scan the QR code below.

FORGING CHAOS EXCERPT

ODIN

I let Thora scribble all over the other group's notes, watching as she mutters to herself the whole time. Class ends and we get our paper back with only a few smiley faces in the margins. I can tell this bothers Thora so I thank Jean and slide the paper in my sweatpants pocket. "Where to now," I ask Thora and she rears her head back in confusion.

"Um, I work."

I frown. I hadn't considered that she had shit to do and wouldn't just come back to my place for more arguments. If I'm really honest, I want her near my bed in case I convince her to join me in it. I scratch my chin. "At the bar?" She nods. I shrug. "I guess I'll be a barfly then. I've never been to a bar during daylight hours…"

She seems confused and I realize I haven't exactly told her that this paper is officially the only thing I have going on until I start physical therapy. "What are you going to do at the bar while I work? Can you drink on your meds?"

"Hey, thanks, Mom." I arch a brow at her while I get myself situated on the knee roller.

She winces. "Sorry. But what are you going to do? Are you seriously going to sit there and bug me?"

"Ah, so I bug you? Sounds interesting." Veins start pulsing in her neck and I laugh. "I'll sit on a bar stool and eat some soup or something and work on our bibliography."

Thora bites her lip, which is probably the only plump thing on her body and I stare as she works her teeth along the rosy, sensitive skin. "I guess that's okay. We're usually pretty slow on the lunch shift."

I start rolling back down Forbes and she walks beside me. "Don't you usually work evenings?"

She sighs. "I work whenever I can get in there. You know I'm moving to the UK this fall, right?" I shake my head. She hums. "Fern and I both are. She's there long term but I'm just there for a year. And I need so much stuff I can't afford yet." She pauses while I navigate a curb cut, successfully this time. "You probably don't care about my airfare or my professional wardrobe."

"I care. I'm not an asshole."

"Oh, no, you're renowned for your benevolence." Thora laughs. "What do they say about you? That you rack people up by the horns or something?"

"Well, nobody's going to say that ever again, are they?"

Thora stares at me with her mouth hanging open. "Oh my god, Odin. I'm so sorry. I keep doing that to you. How can you stand me?"

"I'm not really sure I can," I joke. We get to the bar and she holds the door open. I'm happy to see this place has a ramp in from the curb. I guess the owners want everyone to be able to access their cheap beer and fried food. I make my way to the stool at the end of the bar and Thora walks behind it, tossing her bag somewhere and tugging on a black apron.

"What'll it be, Stag?"

I consider this. She's right about the meds not mixing with liquor. But this place serves all kinds of fried food I'm never allowed to eat while I'm in training. And I'll never have anyone telling me what to eat again. I slap the sticky wood surface of the bar. "Bring me the app platter."

She frowns. "That's meant to serve four people."

"App. Platter." I enunciate each syllable and pop all the p's until Thora laughs and shakes her head. I watch as she types in my order and then hurries to serve some preppy kid who thinks he's cool because he's going to drink with his lunch.

She walks off to pour his beer and I glare at him when he sets a crumpled dollar in a ring of condensation on the bar. He walks off with his beer as Thora heads to the kitchen, presumably for my food, and I reach in my wallet for a five, placing that guy's shitty tip along with my addition on a drink napkin, nice and smooth and dry.

When Thora sets the food in front of me, she sees the tip and a smile spreads wide across her face. She folds the bills neatly and adds them to the jar by the register.

I eat all the fried food, knowing it will make my guts churn. It takes me all of five minutes to type up our sources for our essay, so I take my time and watch her work, conferring with her between customers and adding some stuff to a list in my phone that we can use for our presentation.

I was going to bully her into coming back to my apartment after her shift, but between leaving the house and eating all the heavy food, I'm exhausted. I text my cousins to come get me and leave a twenty folded neatly by my plate.

I force myself to walk away, because if she sees me, she'll refuse the tip and I want her to have it.

Buy Forging Chaos now to keep reading Odin and Thora's story!

ALSO BY LAINEY DAVIS

Stag Brothers Series

Sweet Distraction (Tim and Alice)

Filled Potential (Ty and Juniper)

Fragile Illusion (Thatcher and Emma)

A Stag Family Christmas

Beautiful Game (Hawk and Lucy)

Stag Generations Books

Forging Passion (Wes and Cara prequel)

Forging Glory (Wes and Cara)

Forging Legacy (Wyatt and Fern)

Forging Chaos (Odin and Thora)

Playing for Keeps (Gunnar and ...)

Bridges and Bitters series

Fireball: An Enemies to Lovers Romance (Sam and AJ)

Liquid Courage: A Marriage in Crisis Romance (Chloe and Teddy)

Speed Rail: A Single Dad Romance (Piper and Cash)

Last Call: A Marriage of Convenience Romance (Esther and Koa)

Planted and Plowed series

Against the Grain (Eila and Ben)

The Burgh and the Bees (Eden and Nate)

Yule Be Sorry (Eliza and ???)

Sappy Go Lucky (Eva and Asher)

Since You've Bean Gone (Ethan and Lia) *part of the Farm 2 Forking series

Binge the following series in eBook, paperback, or audio!

Brady Family Series

Foundation: A Grouchy Geek Romance (Zack and Nicole)

Suspension: An Opposites Attract Romance (Liam and Maddie)

Inspection: A Silver Fox Romance (Kellen and Elizabeth)

Vibration: An Accidental Roommates Romance (Cal and Logan)

Current: A Secret Baby Romance (Orla and Walt)

Restoration: A Silver Fox Redemption Romance (Mick and Celeste)

Oak Creek Series

The Nerd and the Neighbor (Hunter and Abigail)

The Botanist and the Billionaire (Diana and Asa)

The Midwife and the Money (Archer and Opal)

The Planner and the Player (Fletcher and Thistle)

Stone Creek University

Deep in the Pocket: A Football Romance

Hard Edge: A Hockey Romance

Possession: A Football Romance

www.ingramcontent.com/pod-product-compliance
Lightning Source LLC
Chambersburg PA
CBHW032158190726
48289CB00007BA/2284